S [illegible]

"Go on," [illegible] Todd, avoiding his [illegible] wouldn't break down. "Get in the car, Todd. They're all waiting."

"You go first," Todd urged her. "I don't want to leave before you do."

Elizabeth nodded. Kissing Todd on the cheek, she turned and took a few tentative steps down the drive. She could feel Todd watching her. *I'll just keep walking,* she told herself. *One foot in front of the other, and by the time I reach the end of the street, they'll be gone. They'll—*

A sudden panic broke over her as Elizabeth realized that this was really it. In just a matter of seconds Todd would be gone. A new flood of tears burst from her as she spun around and ran back up the drive to where Todd was standing with his hand on the car door. "Todd!" she cried, flinging her arms around him. "Oh, Todd, I'm going to miss you so much!"

Bantam Books in the Sweet Valley High Series
Ask your bookseller for the books you have missed

SWEET VALLEY HIGH

SAY GOODBYE

Written by
Kate William

Created by
FRANCINE PASCAL

BANTAM BOOKS
TORONTO · NEW YORK · LONDON · SYDNEY · AUCKLAND

RL 6, IL age 12 and up

SAY GOODBYE
A Bantam Book / October 1985

Sweet Valley High is a trademark of Francine Pascal

Conceived by Francine Pascal

Produced by Cloverdale Press, Inc.,
133 Fifth Avenue, New York, N.Y. 10003

Cover art by James Mathewuse

ISBN 0-553-25176-7

Published simultaneously in the United States and Canada

Bantam Books are published by Bantam Books, Inc. Its trademark,
consisting of the words "Bantam Books" and the portrayal of a rooster,
is Registered in U.S. Patent and Trademark Office and in other
countries. Marca Registrada. Bantam Books, Inc., 666 Fifth Avenue,
New York, New York 10103.

PRINTED IN THE UNITED STATES OF AMERICA

O   0 9 8 7 6 5 4 3 2 1

One

"Elizabeth, if you don't open your door this minute, I'm going to break it down!" Jessica Wakefield wailed. She pounded on her twin's locked bedroom door with both fists.

A moment later the door flew open, and Jessica found herself face-to-face with her twin sister.

"It's no use, Jess," Elizabeth said wearily, stepping aside as her sister walked in and threw herself down on her bed. "I'd really rather be by myself right now."

Jessica shook her head in disbelief, her blue-green eyes wide with wonder. "It isn't true, is it?" she asked. "Is Todd really moving to Vermont?"

Elizabeth wiped her tear-streaked face with a tissue. "It's true," she said. A second later she broke down completely. "Oh, Jess," she sobbed,

"I don't know what I'm going to do without him! I feel like a part of me is dying!"

Jessica stared silently at her twin, her eyes filling with sympathetic tears. She couldn't stand seeing Elizabeth so upset. Her sister meant the world to her, and watching her break down this way made Jessica feel so helpless.

Except for a small mole on her right shoulder, Elizabeth and her twin were identical down to the tiny dimple each showed when she smiled. Both had sun-streaked shoulder-length blond hair, sparkling blue-green eyes, and slender, five-foot-six-inch figures. But there the resemblance ended. Elizabeth was practical and organized, and longed to be a serious writer one day. She liked to concentrate on one thing—and one boy—at a time. Jessica tended to be more excitable. Wherever the action was, Jessica was sure to be right in the middle of it. And over the years Jessica had come to rely on her sister to get her out of the scrapes she was so famous for. The twins' handsome, dark-haired older brother Steven was a big help, too—but Elizabeth was the one Jessica depended on. And she couldn't stand to see her twin looking as distraught as she did right now.

But Jessica could certainly understand it. Elizabeth and Todd—they were practically inseparable! Jessica could barely imagine her twin without her steady boyfriend. Not that she hadn't tried. More than once in the past few months, Jessica had tried to persuade her sister to spend less time with Todd Wilkins. It wasn't that Jessica couldn't see Todd's merits. Before Elizabeth and Todd had started dating steadily, Jessica had been interested in Todd herself. As the twins, Todd was a junior at Sweet Valley High. Brown-haired and attractive, he had warm, coffee-colored eyes and a lean, athletic build. He was one of the best basketball players in the school and a terrific dancer. He was also a warm and sympathetic friend. Jessica had heard Elizabeth itemize Todd's good points so often she knew them all by heart. And deep down Jessica agreed with her sister one hundred percent. But that didn't mean she didn't think Todd was just a tiny bit dull.

Still Jessica wasn't insensitive enough to bring that up then. The news of Mr. Wilkins's transfer must have been a shock to poor Elizabeth. That night, at the school talent show Elizabeth had organized, Todd clued everyone in on the news by reciting a sentimental poem about saying goodbye. Jessica had managed to get the story out of Winston Egbert, whose father was a close friend of Mr. Wilkins. He said that the firm Mr. Wilkins worked for had been hinting about a transfer for some time. Knowing how disruptive it would be for Todd to move during the school year, Mr. Wilkins had done his best to dissuade his boss. But the week before, at his firm's semiannual meeting, Mr. Wilkins was told the move would have to be made—and soon. One of the vice-presidents had already found the Wilkinses a temporary home in a suburb of Burlington. But there were still so many details to iron out—a new school for Todd, a whole new part of the country to get used to—that the Wilkenses had decided to move as soon as they could.

"One week." Elizabeth moaned, her head in her hands. "One miserable week. I just can't believe it, Jess. I can't believe that on Sunday morning he's just going to drive to the airport with them and disappear."

"Maybe he can commute back to Sweet Valley on weekends," Jessica suggested brightly. "I saw this couple on the news who do that. They're both executives, only she lives in California and he lives in New York. And every weekend—"

"Jessica," Elizabeth said fiercely, "Todd and I aren't executives! Do you know how much it costs to get to Vermont? It might as well be New Zealand," she added moodily.

"Well," Jessica said, miffed, "there are always letters. And phone calls. Maybe it won't be that awful, Liz. You two can probably save up enough to visit each other once in a while, and—"

"It isn't the same," Elizabeth interrupted, blinking back tears. "Jess, I've seen Todd every day for so long that I feel like he's a part of me! How am I supposed to just watch him take off? When I think of all the things we'd planned to do together—"

Oh, dear, Jessica thought, watching her twin begin to cry again. *This just won't do at all. I'm going to have to think of some way to cheer her up.*

Jessica couldn't bear seeing someone she loved this depressed. Sitting in her sister's bedroom upstairs in the Wakefields' attractive, split-level house, Jessica tried to put herself in her twin sister's shoes. But she was having a hard time.

In fact, the more Jessica thought about it, the less of a problem Todd's move seemed to be. Elizabeth would miss him for a while, she thought philosophically. But she'd get over it! Then she and Jessica could start going out together again on double dates, looking guys over at the Dairi Burger—having *fun* together again. Jessica just could not convince herself that Todd had been anything other than a drag when it came to her sister's social life.

No, it seemed to Jessica that this was the very best thing that could have happened. All she had to do now was to help Elizabeth realize that.

But from the expression on Elizabeth's face,

5

Jessica had a feeling that it wasn't going to be easy.

"If only there were something I could do!" Elizabeth moaned softly, her face against the woolly material of Todd's sweater. Todd had been out doing errands for his father, and he had dropped by to see Elizabeth before dinner. It was strange how quickly things had changed, Elizabeth thought. A few weeks ago she would have laughed at the thought of squeezing fifteen minutes in with Todd on a weekday afternoon. Now the moments felt precious.

She and Todd were sitting on the front steps of the Wakefields' house, staring moodily at the occasional car driving down the shady side street. Late-afternoon sun brightened the front lawn, but for once Elizabeth was blind to the beauty of her neighborhood. She couldn't imagine sitting out there the following week, knowing there would be no chance that Todd's car might pull into the drive. She couldn't imagine walking into school without Todd there, waiting for her before homeroom. Or eating lunch in the cafeteria without him. Or hanging out on Friday nights at the Dairi Burger alone.

It was impossible. Try as she might to imagine life without Todd, all Elizabeth could conjure up was a feeling of utter desolation and helplessness. There were so many events coming up in the next few weeks that she had planned to go to with Todd. There were the sailboat races in a few weeks. And Lila Fowler's big spring pool party. A double date they'd set up with Roger Patman and his girlfriend, Olivia Davidson. It all seemed bleak without Todd.

But these events weren't what mattered most. More than anything, she would miss the ordinary things: the evening visits she and Todd loved so much, the Saturday afternoons at the beach, the warm feel of Todd's arm around her as they walked through the halls at school. "I don't think I'm going to be able to stand this," Elizabeth murmured.

Todd's brown eyes filled with tears. "I know how you feel, Liz," he whispered. "Remember how we felt when we thought you were moving to San Francisco?"

Elizabeth nodded, a lump in her throat. The twins' mother worked as an interior designer in Sweet Valley, and several months before, she'd been offered an exciting job in San Francisco. Jessica and Elizabeth had been horrified at the prospect. Together they had done everything they could to change their mother's mind. To their relief Mrs. Wakefield had decided to postpone the move. That had been a tense period for Todd and Elizabeth. The thought of being separated had filled them with dread. "But this is much, much worse," Elizabeth pointed out now.

7

"It's so much farther away. Besides, there's no chance in the world that you guys will stay in Sweet Valley."

Even as she spoke, Elizabeth prayed Todd would contradict her. *Say that there is a chance*, she begged him silently. *Tell me that your father might change his mind*.

But Todd's response confirmed her fears. "You're right," he said gloomily. "If my father tried to put this move off any longer, he might lose his job. There's no way he'll change his mind now."

"What did he say about visiting?" Elizabeth asked, fighting back tears.

"I think I might be able to come back with him at the end of the month," Todd said, trying to smile. "Once I've got everything organized at the new school."

The new school, Elizabeth thought dully. She couldn't imagine Todd anywhere other than Sweet Valley High. Whom would it be harder for, she wondered, Todd or her? Todd would have so many strange new things to get used to—a whole new state, a different climate, a different world. That would be hard enough. But for Elizabeth . . . to have to see all the familiar places, do all the usual things without Todd there to make them all enjoyable . . .

She didn't know which was worse. All she

8

knew was that she was going to miss Todd more than she could bear.

"I guess Enid talked to you about the party at the Beach Disco this Saturday," Todd said after a long silence.

Elizabeth nodded. Enid Rollins was her closest friend, and Elizabeth knew that Enid had only the best intentions when she announced that she was throwing a big farewell party at the disco for Todd on Saturday. Enid had been like a sister to Todd, and she wanted to do something to make this painful week easier for him. But Elizabeth could barely stand the thought of a party right now. How in the world could she face all her friends the night before Todd moved? It would be impossible to act as though nothing were wrong. To dance in Todd's arms near the ocean, knowing it was the very last night . . .

"Hey, Liz!" Jessica's cheerful voice called from the open window in her bedroom above them. "Mom says dinner's almost ready!"

"I'll come back over tonight," Todd said reassuringly when he saw the downcast expression on Elizabeth's face. She couldn't help reacting this way, even though she knew it was hard on Todd. Saying goodbye to him now, even for just a few hours, was painful. It reminded her that in just a few short days—"

"Good," Elizabeth murmured, lifting her face

9

for Todd's kiss. She was going to have to act like a good sport, however hard it was. There was nothing she could do to prevent Todd's family from leaving, and she was going to have to get used to the idea—fast.

As far as Elizabeth was concerned, she and Todd still had that one week together. And she was going to spend every single second she could of their remaining time with him.

Because, she thought grimly, waving as Todd started his car, *who knows how long it will be before I see him again after Sunday?*

She had no idea. All she knew was that Todd was leaving and she couldn't do a thing about it. She felt as if the world was about to fall in around her, and all she could do was sit by and watch it happen.

"Alice, this looks superb," Ned Wakefield said, unfolding his napkin and looking appreciatively at the fried chicken his wife had brought to the table.

"Not like dorm food, I'll tell you that much," Steven said with a laugh.

With his dark hair and laughing eyes, the twins' older brother looked like a younger version of Mr. Wakefield. Although he went to school at a nearby college and lived in a dorm, lately he had been spending more time at home.

10

Ordinarily he could always cheer Elizabeth up. But not that night.

"I hope it's OK," Mrs. Wakefield said dubiously, taking her place at the table. "I had to work late tonight, and I'm afraid—"

"It looks great, Mom," Steven assured her. A warm smile flashed between mother and son. Mrs. Wakefield, a slim, honey-blond woman, looked especially attractive that night in a slate-blue dress.

"I don't suppose," Jessica began tentatively, "that this would be the right moment to ask anyone here about a short-term loan? My allowance—"

"I'm glad you brought that up, Jess," Mr. Wakefield said in his firmest lawyer's voice. "I knew there was something I wanted to talk to you about."

"You mean you're going to raise my allowance?" Jessica said hopefully, taking a generous portion of salad.

"Not exactly," Mr. Wakefield told her. "Do you remember anything about using our charge account last month at Lisette's?"

Jessica clapped her hand over her mouth. "I completely forgot," she whispered. "I was going to pay you guys back. I was with Lila Fowler, and I found this adorable matching skirt and blouse, and Lila said, 'Oh, just go ahead and

11

charge it on your parents' account. They let you do that without the card,' and—"

"Lila Fowler," Mr. Wakefield interrupted, "has a millionaire for a father. And you, I'm afraid, do not. So to answer your question about a short-term loan, Jessica: absolutely not. In fact your mother and I have decided that this little bill from Lisette's is going to have to be handled by you. And that's all there is to it."

"But, Daddy . . ." Jessica, looking anguished, turned to her mother for support. "That bill must be for almost a hundred dollars! Where am I ever going to get the money?"

"Have you ever considered where your father and I get *our* money?" Mrs. Wakefield asked mildly.

Jessica blanched. "Well, I guess . . . you work."

Mr. Wakefield laughed. "Clever girl. I thought you never noticed."

"But I can't work!" Jessica shrieked. "I'm still in school!"

"What about after school or on weekends?" Mrs. Wakefield asked. "Steven always had part-time jobs in high school. And you had that job in your father's office."

"Don't remind me," Jessica said mournfully. Several months earlier, Jessica had decided that law was the perfect profession for her. The law-yers on her favorite TV shows all led such exciting and interesting lives. In order to find out first-hand how a law firm worked, Jessica had asked her father for an after-school position with his firm. But instead of fighting court battles and defending innocents against injustice, Jessica had found herself responsible for the office filing and photocopying. Thoroughly bored, she had given up her job—and all desires to become an attorney—within a few weeks. "That was such a short time," Jessica said now. "It doesn't really count."

"Don't ask *us* about counting." Mr. Wakefield chuckled. "*You* can count, Jess. And you could count the day you used our charge without asking permission. The bill came to eighty-seven ninety-five, and I suggest you find a part-time job that fits around your schedule so you can pay us back within a month."

"It won't be so bad," Steven said, grinning at his younger sister. "Maybe all that suffering will strengthen your character, Jess."

"I don't *need* strengthening," Jessica mumbled unhappily. "I need about ninety dollars."

Elizabeth was barely listening to the animated conversation around her. She knew her family was purposely avoiding bringing up the subject of Todd's move. They probably thought she needed to take her mind off the whole thing. But Elizabeth couldn't think of anything else.

Five days more, she thought. Five more days, and Todd would be leaving Sweet Valley forever!

We just can't let that stop our love, she thought with sudden determination. *I don't care how far away he is—I'm not going to let this move destroy the wonderful thing we have together!*

Two

"I hope you're not going to hate the party Saturday night," Enid Rollins said anxiously, lifting a forkful of salad to her mouth. Her large green eyes were thoughtful as she studied the somber expression on her best friend's face.

Elizabeth sighed and shook her head. "I'm sure it will be wonderful, Enid," she said at last. "And you're a great friend to think of it. It'll probably be good for Todd—and me, too. If we were alone on Saturday night, we'd just get too sad for words."

Enid and Elizabeth had found a quiet table in a corner of the cafeteria of Sweet Valley High so they could have a good long talk. Todd was spending the lunch hour in his guidance counselor's office, trying to get his records organized to be sent on to the new school.

"It must be so hard on you two," Enid commiserated.

Elizabeth fiddled with the lid of her yogurt container. "It's not the end of the world," she said, trying to sound sensible, staring down at her tray. "I mean, it isn't like Todd's leaving the country or anything. We'll still be able to call each other, and he thinks he may be able to come back here to visit in a few weeks. And maybe this summer . . ."

"You're so brave, Liz," Enid said sympathetically. "But remember, I'm your best friend. You don't have to put on a good front with me. Tell me how you *really* feel."

"Oh, Enid," Elizabeth cried, tears welling up in her eyes, "it's horrible! I really *do* feel like I ought to be a good sport about the whole thing. But it just seems so hopeless! I'm so frightened that the move may affect the way we feel about each other. And I'm afraid I just couldn't stand that."

"Have you two talked about what you're going to do once you're apart?"

Elizabeth shook her head. "Not really. I think we're both trying to deny that the whole thing's really going to happen. But I know we need to talk. I just hope Todd feels the same way I do."

"Which is how?" Enid prompted, taking a sip of chocolate milk.

Elizabeth looked thoughtful. "I guess I really

16

don't want it to have any effect at all. Oh, sure there'll be changes. There'll have to be! But in all the really important ways, I know I'm going to feel the same way about Todd. And I hope he'll feel the same about me, too."

"Does that mean—" Enid hesitated, trying to think of a tactful way to probe further. "You don't think you'll want to see other people. Is that what you mean?"

"You mean start dating again?" Elizabeth shook her head firmly. "I can't imagine it! No, Enid. That's completely out of the question."

Enid didn't say anything, but the quizzical expression in her eyes made Elizabeth slightly uneasy. She had been sure Enid would understand. Enid of all people ought to have realized that she could never start dating other people—however far away Todd was!

"A lot of couples manage things despite a temporary separation," Elizabeth added defensively. "You'll see, Enid. I bet it doesn't make that much difference once we get used to the whole thing!"

"I'm sure you two will know how to handle it," Enid said soothingly. "I've never known two people with as much common sense as you and Todd."

Elizabeth felt an angry flush creeping up her neck and face. "I know I'm usually practical,

Enid. But at a time like this, being reasonable might be the very worst thing."

"Why?" Enid demanded. "What would you do differently if you were going to be 'reasonable' about the situation?"

Elizabeth bit her lip. "Who knows," she said finally, trying to sound casual. "I'd probably figure that it would be too hard to maintain a steady relationship with someone who's two thousand miles away. Todd and I might decide just to be friends. And that would be a disaster!"

Enid sighed and set her milk carton down. "Well, two thousand miles *is* an awfully long way away, Liz. It's probably different for every couple, but I would have thought—"

"It *is* different for every couple," Elizabeth said hurriedly, as she spotted Todd coming into the cafeteria. She waved him over. "All I know is that *this* couple isn't going to fall apart just because we have to be in different places for a while. I'm not going to lose Todd, Enid. I just can't!"

Enid didn't answer, but Elizabeth didn't like the concerned expression on her best friend's face. *I don't see why she's so doubtful*, she thought unhappily. *Todd and I can definitely make it work!*

But I'd sure feel better if we had some support, she thought. *As it is, it seems like everything's stacked against us. But it doesn't matter. We're going to make it anyway—no matter how hard it seems, or how impractical!*

"How'd the job search go?" Steven asked his sister, affectionately rumpling her blond hair.

Jessica was lying on her stomach on the diving board of the Wakefields' swimming pool, trying to tan the backs of her legs. It was almost five o'clock, but the sun was still strong enough to help maintain her golden tan. "Quit it!" she said crossly, jerking her head out of Steven's reach. "You're wrecking my hair, and I just brushed it!"

"Couldn't tell," Steven joked, sitting down on the edge of the pool and dangling his legs in the water. "It looked awful before I got near it!"

"For your information," Jessica told her brother, "I *got* a job on my very first try. I'm starting on Saturday."

"Don't tell me," Steven said, closing his eyes and tilting his head back so the sun would hit his face. "You're going to work at Lisette's as a sales clerk and take your pay in silk scarves."

"Very funny," Jessica said, miffed. "You'll never guess in a million years." She pulled herself up to a sitting position so she could see her brother's reaction. "I'm going to be a part-time receptionist at the Perfect Match Computer Dating Agency!"

Steven groaned and clapped his hand to his

head. "God save us," he cried. "You're kidding, aren't you?"

"Of course not," Jessica said indignantly. "I think all I get to do is answer phones," she added, "but maybe after a while—"

"I can't believe it," Steven said, shaking his head. "The thought of you working for a dating agency— it's like throwing a lighted match into a tank of gasoline."

"I don't know what you're talking about," Jessica said, twisting a lock of blond hair around one finger, an expression of injured innocence on her face. "Mary Ann—she's the woman who runs the place—says I'm a natural."

"That's exactly what I mean. Actually," Steven added, laughing, "it'll probably be the best thing that ever happened to Sweet Valley. If you concentrate your energy on the people who *want* to be paired off, maybe the rest of us can breathe easy."

"If you're still mad about Cara Walker—" Jessica began.

"Mad?" Steven laughed. "How could I be mad? Would you be mad at whatever caused the great fire of San Francisco? Or the earthquake of sixty-five? Or—"

"You're trying to say it was a disaster," Jessica said coldly. "Well, that wasn't *my* fault. Cara's a perfectly nice girl, Steve. I was only trying to help."

Jessica blinked, fearing she'd gone too far. It had been some time since Tricia Martin, Steven's girlfriend, had died tragically of leukemia. Jessica had only been trying to help during that period, when she suggested he go out with Cara Walker, one of her closest friends. He wasn't ready to be introduced to other girls—not then. And Cara Walker wasn't his type—he'd made that very clear.

But Steven didn't seem upset now by what Jessica had said. "I know you were trying to help," he said softly. A smile spread over his face. "But do me a favor, Jess. Don't help me again! I'm probably better off on my own, just sort of stumbling my way through things as best I can."

Jessica looked appraisingly at her brother as she slipped off the diving board and wrapped a towel around her slim hips. *He's so good-looking*, she mused. And despite what he'd said, he didn't seem to be doing very well on his own. He was still spending far too much time at home, alone!

No, Jessica thought, Steven just didn't know what was good for him. Guys were almost always that way. Apparently Cara Walker wasn't Steven's type, but that didn't mean Jessica couldn't find someone who was.

Especially, she thought as she walked across the patio and opened the door to the house, now that she had Mary Ann and the Perfect Match computer to help her out!

"Can I come in?" Steven asked gently, putting his head inside Elizabeth's room.

Elizabeth was staring blankly at her notebook, trying to piece together a paragraph in a story she was working on for *The Oracle*, the school newspaper at Sweet Valley High. "Sure, Steve," she said, trying to smile. "I'm afraid the creative juices just aren't flowing this afternoon."

Steven sat down on her bed, looking affectionately at the photographs decorating his sister's dresser and bookshelves. Todd was in almost all of them.

"You're really going to miss him, aren't you?" he said at last.

Elizabeth nodded. She wished she could tell Steven how awful she felt at the thought of Todd's moving so far away. But it seemed tactless. *Imagine how Steve must have felt when Tricia was dying*, she reminded herself. *He* couldn't console himself with the prospect of reunions. It was over so quickly, and it was over forever.

"Do you want to talk about it?" Steven asked gently. "I know sometimes it makes it better to talk—and sometimes it just makes it worse."

Elizabeth's lower lip trembled. "I wouldn't mind talking," she admitted. "I just feel guilty, that's all. It seems like such a small thing—"

"Small?" Steven's eyebrows shot up. "It doesn't seem small to me. You and Todd have known each other for ages. And you've been practically inseparable. I'd think it's going to be awfully hard for you two to be apart."

Elizabeth blinked back tears. "It *is* hard," she admitted. "It's kind of weird even now, when we both know we should be enjoying our last few days together. Everything we do—like going to the Dairi Burger or going to the beach—has this awful finality about it. We both keep thinking, 'Well, I guess that's the last time we do *that*.' "

"I know," Steven said softly. "There's nothing worse than being conscious something is coming to an end—especially when that 'something' is very special."

"But it isn't really coming to an end," Elizabeth said hurriedly. "I mean, the kind of inseparable friendship we've had—that's got to end. But Todd and I are going to keep in touch as much as we can. There'll be phone calls, and letters, and it looks like a few visits. So—"

"Liz, can I ask you a question? Are you and Todd planning on keeping things just as they are now after the move?"

"What do you mean?" Elizabeth asked. "Do you mean, are we going to date other people and all that?"

Steven smiled. "I guess that *is* what I meant."

Elizabeth shook her head. "We haven't really talked about it, but I know that neither one of us wants to. I know it's going to be hard, but we feel—"

"I don't suppose I can give you a word of brotherly advice," Steven said. "This may not be the best time to bring it up, but I don't know if that's such a good idea, Liz."

Elizabeth bit her lip. First Enid, now Steven. Couldn't they see that this was what was best for Todd and her? She didn't want people telling her how hard it was going to be. She and Todd already knew that!

"I've seen this sort of thing a lot at college," Steven went on. "People have what they call 'hometown honeys'—girlfriends or boyfriends they've left behind. And the ones who have the hardest time always seem to be the ones whose expectations and demands are too high. They promise not to date, not to spend any time with the opposite sex at all. And they get really jealous if there's even a hint that they're being cheated on. It's the surest way I know to wreck a good friendship."

"I'm sure that's true in a lot of cases, Steve," Elizabeth said a bit defensively, "but the way Todd and I feel, any other agreement would be ridiculous! I'm not saying that I won't see my friends after Todd's gone. And a lot of my friends are guys. But dating—or getting involved

24

with someone else—I just can't imagine it happening."

"Well," Steven said finally, getting to his feet and flashing Elizabeth a special smile, "I've never worried about you when it comes to making decisions, Liz. You've got both feet on the ground. However hard it is for you and Todd, I know you two will work it out. And you'll do what's right for both of you."

Elizabeth stared at her brother, wishing she could smile back. He looked about as convinced of that as Enid had, she thought miserably. Everyone seemed to think that she and Todd were going to ruin their lives just because they refused to let distance ruin their love!

But she wasn't going to change her mind, Elizabeth vowed, no matter what everyone else thought was wisest.

No matter what happened, she told herself, Todd and she were a twosome. And that was the way it was going to stay.

Three

It was Saturday afternoon, and Jessica was alone in the plush front office of the Perfect Match Agency. Mary Ann had gone out for a late lunch, leaving Jessica in charge. "Just answer the phone when it rings and take a message," the pert brunette had instructed.

"What a bore," Jessica said to herself. So far, working for a dating agency wasn't proving to be very interesting. For half an hour that morning Jessica had felt very glamorous, twisting around in her swivel chair and taking messages on a heart-shaped notepad with a freshly sharpened pencil. But by ten o'clock she was a little disillusioned. Somehow Jessica had been sure all the calls would be from terribly attractive men, but most of them seemed to be women—all desperate to find out if their dates for that night had come through. "Just keep track of all the new ones," Mary Ann instructed blithely, filing her nails. "Enter their names on index cards and put them in the top drawer. We'll get to them eventually."

What a waste of available women, Jessica thought crossly, writing down the dozenth name and number on a pink, three-by-five card. *Just think— Steve could be reaping the benefits of my new job, and I wouldn't even have to enter his name in the computer. I could just give his name and number to the next five women who call!*

It was a tempting idea. But having considered it for a few minutes, Jessica decided it wouldn't be fair to Steven to match him up with just anybody. She would sneak into Mary Ann's back files, she thought excitedly, and find women who really seemed right for Steven. Then she could call them and tell them the computer had just come up with the perfect man, someone who matched their interests in every way— Steven Wakefield!

Jessica was about to open the bottom file drawer in Mary Ann's private office when the door swung open. "What are you doing, Jessica?" Mary Ann asked pleasantly, slipping out of her jacket.

Jessica gulped. "I—uh, I wanted to look through some old profiles so I could get a better idea of what the agency is all about."

Mary Ann grinned. "Why? You're not interested in being matched up by the computer, are you?"

"Who knows?" she said airily. "No, I just hoped I could do a better job here if I knew more about the way the agency works," she said smoothly.

"That's very admirable, Jessica." Her boss smiled. "But I really need you to cover the phones right now. Why don't I give you keys to the office? That way you can come back whenever you like and read the files to your heart's content."

Jessica's eyes lit up. "That would be wonderful," she said sincerely. A minute later Mary Ann had slipped a set of keys into her hands— dangling, as Jessica had suspected, from a heart-shaped key ring.

"Don't lose them," Mary Ann warned. "We wouldn't want just *anyone* getting hold of our private files. Who knows what could happen?"

Yes, Jessica thought silently, tucking the keys deep in her pocket. *Who knows indeed!*

Much to her surprise, the rest of the afternoon went quickly. Mary Ann was fun to work with. About twenty-seven, she had started the agency with her older sister and now ran it herself. She was vivacious and pretty, her brown curls framing a lovely oval face. By the end of the afternoon, Jessica found herself confiding in Mary Ann as if she were an old friend, like Cara

Walker or Lila Fowler. When Mary Ann asked her what her plans were for the night, Jessica began just by mentioning the party Enid was throwing at the Beach Disco. But by four o'clock she had told her boss all about Elizabeth and Todd.

"Frankly," Jessica admitted, chewing thoughtfully on the end of one of Mary Ann's pink pencils, "I think it's the best thing that could have happened to the two of them. They haven't realized that they're getting stale as a couple, but they are, I can just tell. Elizabeth refuses to go *anywhere* without Todd. You'd think he was her shadow! And when I suggest something like going to a party without him—or even *thinking* about another guy—Liz acts like I'm trying to infect her or something!"

"Well, she and Todd must be happy together," Mary Ann said gently.

"She's wasting her youth," Jessica said. "Besides," she added after a moment's consideration, "Todd isn't really that good for Liz. I think they're too much alike. They're both—well, you know—sensible, thoughtful, kind—all that."

"What's wrong with that?" Mary Ann laughed. "It sounds ideal! A model couple. We should use them to advertise our agency!"

Jessica shook her head. "It's too much of a good thing. That's what the problem is. They're both great on their own, but together—*bo-ring!* No, I'm sure Liz could do much better."

"And she's never gone out with anyone else the whole time she's been dating Todd?" Mary Ann inquired.

Jessica thought for a minute. "Not really," she said. "There was Nicholas Morrow for a little while, but she didn't really go *out* with him. He was crazy about her, but she never gave him much of a chance."

"Who's Nicholas Morrow?" Mary Ann asked.

"Nicholas Morrow," Jessica said, "is simply the best-looking, richest, most amazing guy. He's eighteen, and he lives in one of those huge mansions up on the hill. His father's an absolute *millionaire,* and Nicholas is *fabulous.* He's got dark hair and incredible green eyes and the best body—and Liz told him she was really in love with Todd and asked if they could just be friends. I almost died."

Actually Jessica had been interested in Nicholas herself when the Morrows first moved to Sweet Valley. If he'd shown the slightest interest in her, she would *never* have been as stupid as she thought Elizabeth had been about the whole thing. As it was, all she could do was fume at her twin every now and then about how she'd turned down what would have been a ticket to everlasting wealth and happiness.

"Will Nicholas be at the disco tonight? Maybe

you can convince him *you're* the one for him, not Elizabeth," Mary Ann suggested.

"No." Jessica sighed. "It's a lost cause." She had tried her hardest to get Nicholas to notice her, but there just wasn't a *chance* of making it happen. No, it looked as if Nicholas Morrow was lost to the Wakefields forever.

Unless, Jessica thought suddenly, *I can convince Nicholas that Elizabeth needs cheering up after Todd moves!*

She might have turned him down once, Jessica told herself—but that was while Todd was there to badger Elizabeth every second. Once he was good and far away . . .

Nicholas and Elizabeth! she thought. What a wonderful pair they'd be.

Elizabeth Wakefield, she thought, her eyes sparkling with determination, *I'm not going to let you shrivel up or pine away. Nicholas and I are going to save you from everlasting sorrow!*

"Doesn't Liz look beautiful?" Jessica whispered to Nicholas, looking across the crowded dance floor to where her twin was dancing dreamily in Todd's arms.

"She sure does," Nicholas admitted.

Actually, Nicholas was the one Jessica kept looking at. He looked even more handsome than usual that night in a navy blazer and crisp white shirt. He was so much more *sophisticated* than

anyone her age was, Jessica thought appreciatively. So much more *distinguished*.

"You know, Nicholas," Jessica said confiden-
tially, dropping her voice a little, "I bet Liz
would really appreciate some company once
Todd's moved. She'll probably be feeling a little
low for a few days. I'm sure she'd love having
your support."

Nicholas's eyebrows shot up. "She doesn't
look like she's going to want company," he
pointed out. "Not for a long time, I'd say—if
ever!"

Jessica laughed merrily. "Of course she
doesn't *look* like it," she whispered. "How could
she? This is a farewell party for Todd, after all.
But just give it a few days," she added. "After
all, Nicholas, you're such a good friend of hers.
And soon Liz will be needing her friends more
than ever—if you see what I mean."

"Thanks, Jess," Nicholas said, looking at
Elizabeth with interest. "I appreciate the tip."

Jessica nodded in satisfaction as she watched
Nicholas stroll over to the bar where Enid Rollins
and Winston Egbert were standing. The more
she thought about it, the better she felt about the
idea of Nicholas and Elizabeth together. What
would have been *best*, of course, Jessica
reflected, would have been Nicholas falling in
love with *her*. But as things stood, Nicholas

would be a thousand times better for Elizabeth than Todd.

He was exactly what she needed, Jessica thought. Someone a little older, someone with a different perspective. Someone *new*. And most of all, someone who *wasn't* moving to Vermont!

Actually, now that Todd was moving, Jessica felt kind of fond of him. She had to admit he looked good that night, too—almost as good as Nicholas. Todd had his good points, that was for sure. But he and Elizabeth were like bread and butter. They were good together but just so *boring*! They just didn't make sparks fly anymore. Clearly Todd's move was just the opportunity her twin needed to expand her horizons. And once Jessica helped Elizabeth see it that way, she could stop looking so mournful and start having a good time again.

That was all there was to it, Jessica thought. Someone had to save Elizabeth before she ended up in a convent or something. And Nicholas was definitely the one to do it.

"Todd, let's sit this one out," Elizabeth whispered as the band started up again. "I feel like we've barely had a chance to talk all night. And tomorrow—"

"Let's go outside," Todd said huskily. "I feel like looking at the water with you one last time. We can talk out there."

A minute later the two of them had slipped outside. The cool night air felt wonderful. Elizabeth was glad to be alone with Todd, away from the crowded disco. "It's gorgeous out here," she said, looking up at the moon as they walked on the beach.

"Liz . . ." Todd whispered, turning to face her.

Suddenly they were in each other's arms. Elizabeth could feel Todd's heart pounding as he clutched her to him. She could hear him whispering her name over and over again as his lips searched for hers in the darkness. The next minute his warm mouth was touching hers, and she could feel the wetness of his face as tears streamed from his eyes.

"Come with me," he said soberly, taking her hand and leading her across the damp sand.

Elizabeth hadn't been out by the water at night for a long time. Squeezing Todd's hand, she walked with him along the line where the tide was coming in and listened to the waves crashing over the sand. But Elizabeth was only half-conscious of the sounds and sensations around her—the damp sand in her sandals, the smell of saltwater, the moonlight sparkling on the water. All she could think of was how close Todd was right then . . .

"Liz," Todd said earnestly, taking a folded piece of tissue paper from the breast pocket of his blazer, "I have something for you. It's nothing much," he added hastily, seeing the expression on her face. "I just wanted you to have a little remembrance that you could wear all the time."

Fumbling with the tissue paper, Elizabeth unwrapped a tiny gold locket on a fine chain. "It's beautiful," she murmured, tears in her eyes. "Todd, I'll never take it off."

Todd stared sadly at the ground. "My father and I had a long talk last night, Liz. He thinks it's selfish of me to try to have claims on you from so far away. He told me I should encourage you to meet other guys. But I—"

"I know." Elizabeth sighed. "I've heard the same argument from just about everyone—my parents, Steve, even Enid! But I don't see why we should listen to them. All we can do is follow what our hearts tell us, Todd. And if you feel the way I do, then—"

"I do," Todd interrupted, pulling Elizabeth closer to him. "I just can't imagine holding another girl like this. If you can just be patient . . ."

"I don't want anyone but you." Elizabeth wept, holding Todd as tightly as she could. "How can anyone else tell us what's best, anyway? We're the only ones who know how we feel!"

"I'm so glad you agree," Todd murmured.

"God, Liz, if I thought you were in love with someone else . . . if I had to carry on from day to day a couple of thousand miles away, knowing you wanted some other guy . . .

"I'll write every day," Todd told her. "And I'm going to get a part-time job right away so I can afford to call you often. And so I can start saving to come back for a visit as soon as I can."

"Oh, Todd," Elizabeth said with a sob, her face against his shoulder, "I love you so much! I don't think I'm going to be able to stand this!"

"I love you, too," Todd whispered. "I guess all we can do is hang on and be strong, Liz—and ignore all the advice our families are giving us. We're too much in love to forget each other just because we're far apart."

"I could never forget you," Elizabeth cried emphatically, tears streaming down her cheeks.

She had no idea how she was going to survive the next twenty-four hours. All she knew was that she was going to have to, somehow, even though right then it felt as if her heart were breaking.

Elizabeth felt as if she were in the middle of a terrible nightmare. *But this is real,* she told herself miserably. *There's no way I can put an end to what's happening by waking up.* There was nothing she could do at all.

Four

It was Sunday afternoon, and Jessica was kneeling in front of the big file cabinet in Mary Ann's office, riffling through the profiles the agency had received over the last few weeks. Jessica had let herself in with her new set of keys and gone straight to work trying to find recent applicants who had not yet received the names of men to contact.

Each file contained a questionnaire, filled out in detail by the applicant, and a pink index card with various notes Mary Ann had jotted down. There were no photographs, and Jessica was spending ages agonizing over the folders, trying to decide what each woman was like. One was "tall, cheerful, and athletic," which sounded pretty good, but she wanted a man over forty-five, preferably a doctor. Another was "blond, slim, and fond of the out-of-doors," but she wanted "a man willing to relocate to Italy," and Jessica didn't think Steven would go for that.

At last Jessica had a list of prospective matches. Beatrice Barber, the first one, was a little on the old side—forty-three, her application said. But she was self-described as "beautiful, energetic, and a lot of fun." What was there to object to in that? And she was divorced from "a wealthy banker," so she probably had a lot of money to throw around. Besides, Jessica thought, Steven might do well with an older woman. According to the *National Enquirer*, it was a good move. All the stars thought so.

Next on the list was Jordan MacGuire, whose name Jessica thought was terribly glamorous. She was interested in "films, foreign accents, sports cars, and German philosphers." Her nickname was Jody, and she was only twenty—just a little bit older than Steven. Jessica thought this was an inspired choice. Steven was always bragging about how much he'd learned since he'd been away at college, and this Jody sounded as though she'd be a worthy companion. Maybe they could go to coffeehouses together and get extremely intellectual.

The only other candidate Jessica found who really seemed worth pursuing was a woman named Melissa Porter. Her nickname was Missy, and according to her questionnaire, she loved "cooking, restaurants, eating—as well as all sorts of traditional things around the house." Steven had been making such a big deal about how lousy dormitory food was—maybe Melissa would fall in love with him and cook wonderful meals for him. *That* would make him happy.

Satisfied for the time being, Jessica closed the file cabinet and hurried back to the desk in the lobby with the three names and telephone numbers. Settling back in her swivel chair, she dialed the first number.

"Ms. Barber? This is the Perfect Match Computer Dating Agency, and I just wanted to let you know that our computer has just come up with the man of your dreams!"

"Really?" a middle-aged voice inquired. "That was quick! Can you tell me anything about him? What's his name?"

"His name," Jessica said dramatically, "is *Steven Wakefield*. And I'd be happy to satisfy your curiosity about him. But I think the best thing would be for me to give you his telephone number, so you can find out for yourself how wonderful he really is. Only don't mention where you got his name, OK? He's a little shy about using our agency—since he's *so* gorgeous!"

What a wonderful sister I am, Jessica thought happily. In no time at all Steven would have a new girlfriend. She didn't want him to be overwhelmed, though. She'd wait to see what happened with the first woman before she made any other calls. But one of them was bound to make him forget Tricia Martin once and for all!

Elizabeth was sitting on the front steps of the Wilkinses' house, watching the family loading the car with suitcases. "What's going to happen?" Elizabeth asked miserably. "You can't just leave the house—and all this furniture!"

"Mr. Egbert is going to take care of selling the house for us," Mr. Wilkins explained, patting Elizabeth on the shoulder as if to show he knew how she felt. "We expect it may take a few months, but Sam knows what he's doing."

Sam Egbert was a realtor and the father of Winston, a classmate of Elizabeth and Todd generally known as the school clown. Usually Elizabeth burst out laughing when she thought about Winston and his antics. But this afternoon nothing could make her smile.

"But what about the furniture?" she pressed stubbornly. It was as if she thought she could remind the Wilkinses of some terrible oversight and keep them right there in Sweet Valley.

"Sam is going to have it shipped to us along with the car once we've wrapped up the deal on the house my firm is looking at," Mr. Wilkins told her. Todd had sold his own car, a blue Datsun, a day earlier.

Elizabeth bit her lip. Everything seemed so final, so irreversible.

"Don't worry, Liz," Mr. Wilkins said fondly, lowering his voice so Todd couldn't hear him. "I expect you'll be seeing more of your friend here than you think."

Elizabeth nodded numbly. She barely heard what Todd's father had said. She just hoped her expression belied what she was feeling inside. It hurt even to look at Todd; his face was so full of the emotions she was feeling. She was afraid if she met his gaze she'd burst into tears in front of the whole family.

"OK, Todd," Mr. Wilkins said finally, wiping his brow as he surveyed the contents of the car. "If we're going to make it to the airport in time to get on our flight, we've got to pull out of here in ten minutes. And I have a hunch there's someone you'd rather spend those ten minutes with than your aging father."

"Come on, Liz," Todd muttered, grabbing her arm.

Tears blinding her eyes, Elizabeth jumped to her feet and followed Todd. She could barely see where she was going. All she knew was that Todd's fingers were grasping her arm. He was still there, still beside her. Ten more minutes, and . . .

"Let's go out back," Todd whispered, slipping his arm around her waist. Elizabeth nodded, smiling gratefully up into his brown eyes. She was so glad Todd had thought to take her away

41

so they could be by themselves for a few minutes. It was so hard in front of his family, so difficult to keep from sobbing.

"Last night," Todd whispered, his voice thick, "I told myself that I'd be brave for your sake. I said—" His voice broke, and he looked away from Elizabeth, fighting for control. "I told myself that I wouldn't cry. But, Liz . . ."

The next minute tears were running down his cheeks.

As much as she had thought about it Elizabeth had no idea their parting would be so painful. Tears fell from her own eyes as she stared at Todd's sorrowful face. The next minute she was in his arms, crying as if she'd never stop, her chest heaving against his.

It seemed to Elizabeth that they had only held each other for an instant when she heard Todd's father calling. "I've got to go," Todd said, lifting his tear-streaked face and staring at her as if he were trying to memorize her features.

"Will you call me?" Elizabeth choked out, brushing the tears from her eyes.

Todd nodded. Taking Elizabeth's hand, he walked with her around the side of the house back to the front yard. Elizabeth stared at the car waiting in the front drive. *In just a minute Todd will be in that car*, she told herself. *It'll back down the drive and turn down the street and disappear. And*

Todd won't live here anymore. I won't be able to see him tonight. Or tomorrow night. Or . . .

"Go on," she whispered to Todd, avoiding his eyes so she wouldn't break down again. "Get in the car, Todd. They're all waiting."

"You go first," Todd urged her. "I don't want to leave before you do."

Elizabeth nodded. Kissing Todd on the cheek and waving at the Wilkinses, who were inside the car, she turned and took a few tentative steps down the drive. She could feel Todd watching her. *I'll just keep walking,* she told herself. *One foot in front of the other, and by the time I reach the end of the street, they'll be gone. They'll—*

A sudden panic broke over her as Elizabeth realized that this was really it. In just a matter of seconds Todd would be gone. A new flood of tears burst from her as she spun around and ran back up the drive to where Todd was standing with his hand on the car door. "Todd!" she cried, flinging her arms around him. "Oh, Todd, I'm going to miss you so much!"

In the end it was Todd who left first. Elizabeth couldn't leave him until he got in the car—and she wouldn't leave the Wilkinses' drive until the last glimpse of the familiar car had vanished around the corner, leaving her entirely alone.

"I'm home!" Jessica announced loudly, slamming the front door behind her and dumping her jacket and bag on the table in the Wakefields' front hall. Nobody answered, and after a minute Jessica headed through the back of the house to the sliding door leading out to the patio, where she found her parents deep in conversation with Steven.

"I thought you were going back to college this afternoon," Jessica said, looking at her brother in confusion.

"Trying to get rid of me?" Steven said lightly. "I'm going back tonight," he added, "but I thought I'd stick around for a while so I could spend some time with Liz before I go."

"That's what we're talking about, Jess," Mr. Wakefield explained. "Your sister's over at the Wilkinses' house right now. I think she's going to need a lot of attention when she gets back."

"*Oh,*" Jessica said, remembering. "The big move is today!"

"That's right," Mrs. Wakefield said. "Jess, has Liz talked to you much about it? We're worried that she's kept awfully quiet about the whole thing."

"Maybe she doesn't care that much," Jessica suggested. "Maybe she's kind of relieved Todd's moving, and she's afraid to admit it."

"I don't think so," Steven said. "What gives you that impression?"

Jessica shrugged. "Well . . ."

Alice Wakefield shook her head. "You may

44

feel that way, honey, but I don't think your sister does. I think she's broken up about the whole thing."

Jessica sighed. "Well, we'll just have to keep her busy," she remarked. "After all—"

"Ssshh!" Steven warned. "I think I hear Liz coming."

A moment later Elizabeth came out onto the patio. Jessica took a deep breath when she saw her twin. She'd never seen Elizabeth looking like this before. From a distance, it was the same old Elizabeth—blond ponytail, neat khaki shorts and polo shirt, grayish tennis shoes with clean laces. But her face . . . Jessica couldn't get over the expression on her twin's face. Her eyes were swollen from crying, and her skin was blotchy. But the worst, the very worst, was the apathetic look in her blue-green eyes. She looked numb.

"Are you OK?" Mrs. Wakefield asked, jumping up to put her arms around her daughter.

Elizabeth nodded stonily. "I wanted to let you all know that I'm fine," she said flatly. "But I'm feeling a little tired, so I thought I'd say goodbye to Steven now and go up and lie down, if that's OK."

"Aren't you going to want any dinner?" Mrs. Wakefield asked, her brow furrowing with concern.

Elizabeth shook her head. "No, thanks," she said quietly.

Jessica stared at her twin in disbelief. This was worse than she feared—much worse! She'd better do something right away. No dinner! This was *serious*!

But I won't let Elizabeth do this to herself, Jessica thought. *No way. Between Nicholas Morrow and me, we just may be able to save her.*

Five

"Thank goodness we have our own car!" Jessica exclaimed, turning the twins' red Fiat Spider down a shady side street en route to Sweet Valley High. It was Monday morning, a week after Todd had left, and Jessica was running through a mental checklist of all the things she had to get done that week: cheerleading practice; two more afternoons at the dating service; and shopping for a new dress for Lila's party that month—even though that meant she'd have to work that much longer to pay back her parents, it would have been impossible to get everything done without the help of the trusty Fiat the twins' parents had given them.

"Mmm," Elizabeth mumbled, scanning a piece of paper covered with her neat hand-writing.

"What's that?" Jessica asked suspiciously. "Something for *The Oracle*?"

Elizabeth bit her lip. As the writer of the "Eyes and Ears" column for the school paper, she had a big commitment to fulfill each week. Ordinarily her assignments were done well ahead of time. Mr. Collins, who taught English and was the advisor for the paper, was Elizabeth's favorite teacher. She couldn't imagine letting him, or her readers, down.

But this past week she'd let her newspaper work slide. It had been eight days since Todd had moved, and Elizabeth had spent every spare minute writing to him. The piece of paper she was holding now was part of the letter she'd begun the night before. At Jessica's query she hastily tucked it back inside her notebook. She didn't want Jessica to know what it was.

"Oh, it's nothing," she said, pretending to concentrate on the lush scenery of the surrounding neighborhood as Jessica stepped on the gas pedal.

"Another letter to Todd?" Jessica asked, her eyes on the road.

Elizabeth sighed. "Yeah," she admitted. "I was hoping to get it to the post office during lunch. But—"

"Liz," Jessica said firmly, glancing in the rearview mirror, "you can't spend your lunch hours running to the post office! Why don't you just give Daddy the letters and let him mail them from his office like we always do?"

"It takes almost a whole day longer that way," Elizabeth said stubbornly. "I asked at the post office. Besides—"

"You don't think Daddy would read your mail!" Jessica exclaimed, giving her twin a side-long glance.

Elizabeth shook her head. "Of course not," she murmured. "I just—" She hesitated. "I just feel better taking it myself. I know it's stupid, but"—Elizabeth blinked back tears—"somehow I feel closer to him if I take the letters myself," she whispered.

Boy, Jessica thought, *she really is far gone. I can't believe this!*

"Why don't we go see a movie sometime this week?" Jessica suggested, pulling the car into the school parking lot. "We haven't done anything like that together in ages."

Elizabeth smiled. "I don't know, Jess. I've got all this stuff to do for *The Oracle*, and—"

"Todd might call," Jessica finished for her.

Elizabeth bit her lip. Her twin was closer to the truth than she might have guessed. So far Todd had called three times—three wonderful phone calls that stood out from the rest of the past week like brilliant points of light in pitch darkness.

Elizabeth had anticipated that the separation was going to be bad, but she didn't think either

49

she or Todd had known exactly how hard it was going to be. Every day—almost every minute—Elizabeth was reminded of Todd in some insignificant way that brought back a flood of warm memories. Passing the gym, for example, she'd catch sight of someone shooting baskets, and she'd remember all those afternoons cheering for Todd as he rushed across the court. When she opened her locker, she saw the coded message Todd had written on the inside of the door. It wouldn't have made sense to anyone but Elizabeth, who knew it meant "I love you." There was nothing Elizabeth did—and no place she went—that didn't remind her of Todd. She had never missed anyone so much in her entire life.

Without Todd, the things Elizabeth had loved to do seemed suddenly hollow. What fun was there in writing the gossip column for the paper, without Todd around to contribute ideas or laugh at her jokes? What fun was studying, without Todd around to talk things over? The thought of going to see a movie without him made a lump form in Elizabeth's throat. She honestly didn't feel like doing much of anything these days. All day at school she watched the clock, longing for the last bell and the chance to go home to see if she'd gotten a letter from Todd. And only when she was writing a letter to him did her terrible loneliness subside. As always, Elizabeth was able to lose herself in her writing.

As she poured out her thoughts and feelings, it actually seemed as if Todd were beside her, listening sympathetically. It seemed—

"Hey," Jessica said suddenly, interrupting her twin's reverie. "You look like you're a million miles away! What's going on!"

Not a million, Elizabeth thought sadly, gathering her books and opening the car door as her twin slipped the keys in the pocket of her jeans. *A couple thousand is more like it. About the distance from here to Burlington, Vermont.*

"I *said*, do you want to have lunch together today?" Jessica demanded, looking miffed.

Elizabeth shook her head, her blond ponytail swinging back and forth. "No, thanks," she said vaguely, looking across the parking lot to the place where Todd used to wait for her every morning. "Thanks anyway, Jess, but—"

"Don't tell me." Jessica groaned. "You and Todd have arranged to send each other messages by mental telepathy every day at noon, right?"

Elizabeth barely noticed the mocking tone in her sister's voice. All she could think about was getting through another day of school without Todd—a long, dismal day to suffer through until she could get home.

I don't know, she worried to herself, oblivious to the concerned expression on Jessica's face. *Maybe I can make it through today, But what about tomorrow—and all the tomorrows after that?*

She didn't know how she was going to make it till the summer, when Todd might be able to come back to Sweet Valley. But Elizabeth couldn't let herself think about that right now. All she could do was steer herself numbly from day to day and pray that somehow this terrible loneliness might ease up.

Because if it doesn't, she told herself miserably, *I think I'm going to die!*

"I don't blame Liz one little bit," Cara Walker announced, crumpling up her bag of potato chips and licking the salt from her fingers. "I'm sure I'd act exactly the way she is. I think you're being incredibly insensitive, Jess."

Jessica and Cara were sitting at a table on the patio outside the cafeteria, finishing their lunches. Jessica, who never had to worry about her weight, was concentrating on her ice-cream sundae, her aqua eyes serious as she reflected on her twin's behavior.

"You're wrong, Cara," she decided finally. "Liz has gone completely off the deep end. It's not that I don't understand how she feels," she added hastily. "I mean, I can see how she misses Todd and everything. But, Cara, she's acting like a widow or something! Does she think she can spend the rest of high school writing letters to Todd? It's ridiculous!"

Cara bit her lip. "You're not being fair," she

insisted. "How else is she supposed to react? She must be so lonely!"

"That's the whole point," Jessica agreed, pushing her sundae away. "She's terribly lonely. And it's up to me to think of some way to help her."

Boy, Cara sure wasn't acting like herself, Jessica thought, sneaking another look at her friend's pretty face. She used to be so much fun—always the first one to know all the gossip, the first to see the joke in everything. Jessica knew Cara's parents were having problems, but she'd never expected Cara to change so much because of it. First Liz, now Cara. Everyone she knew was massively depressed!

"Maybe she just needs to be left alone for a while," Cara suggested quietly.

Jessica's eyebrows shot up as she looked at her closest friend with surprise. Cara was really flipping out. Was she trying to suggest Jessica was interfering—with her very own twin? "What's eating you?" she demanded irritably. "You seem really grouchy today."

Cara's eyes filled with tears. "Oh, it's nothing," she murmured, looking away. "My dad moved out," she said. The look in her eyes clearly said, *and that's all I want to say about it right now*. "But I still think Liz has a right to act how she feels," she added firmly. "Just give her some

53

time, Jess. She'll find a way to come to terms with it."

Jessica looked at Cara. *How does she know?* she wondered. A few weeks ago Jessica would have burst out laughing at such a suggestion. But Cara was so moody these days she didn't know what to say.

"Well, thanks for the diagnosis," Jessica ventured. "But all the same, I think Liz is acting loony. And I intend to save her before she locks herself up in her room forever."

Cara's pretty face tightened. "Well, she's *your* sister," was all she said.

Jessica sighed. She was surrounded by crazy people!

"Actually," she said briskly, "I have an idea that just may help Liz to get out of the doldrums."

"What sort of idea?" Cara asked suspiciously.

"You know how much Liz looks up to Mr. Collins—" Jessica began.

"You're not going to tell me that you think Liz and Mr. Collins—" Cara began, her brown eyes wide with horror.

Jessica burst out laughing. "Of course not!" she assured her friend. "All I'm going to do is ask Mr. Collins to give Liz a special assignment for the newspaper—a really big project that'll get her out of her room and make her stay involved with things at school."

"That sounds like a pretty good idea," Cara said slowly, looking searchingly into Jessica's face. *Too good an idea*, she thought. It didn't sound like the sort of plan Jessica Wakefield usually cooked up.

"It *is* a good idea!" Jessica exclaimed, bouncing up from the table. "In fact, I'm going to try to find Mr. Collins now and see if he can talk to Liz about it this afternoon."

Of course, Jessica hadn't told Cara what made the plan really good. If Mr. Collins could get Elizabeth to cover the big sailing races on Saturday—and if Elizabeth agreed to do it—Jessica knew a contestant who'd be eager for a private interview after the regatta.

Nicholas Morrow was one of the favorites in the race. And with just a little bit of string-pulling, Jessica had a feeling that this coming weekend was going to be her chance to get Elizabeth out of her room and onto Nicholas Morrow's boat. *Or at least*, she thought, smiling, *into his arms!*

"I thought you were coming home straight after school," Jessica said innocently, brushing her blond hair in front of the mirror hanging over Elizabeth's dresser.

Elizabeth turned a page in the book she was reading. "Oh, Mr. Collins asked me to stay after class for a few minutes. He wants me to cover the sailing races this weekend."

Jessica's eyes lit up. "That's wonderful!" she exclaimed.

"Why?" Elizabeth asked curiously, narrowing her eyes. "Since when are you so keen on journalism, Jess?"

Jessica shrugged. "I'm just glad you're getting involved in things around here again, that's all."

Elizabeth sighed. "I really don't feel like doing the story, to tell you the truth," she admitted. "If Mr. Collins hadn't been so insistent, I think I would have turned it down."

"You'll do an excellent job," Jessica said firmly, plopping down on her sister's bed and pretending to think something over. "Who are you going with?" she asked finally.

"Going with where?" Elizabeth asked absentmindedly, turning back to her book.

"Elizabeth Wakefield, do you realize you've been treating me like a ghost for the past ten days!" Jessica shrieked. "I said, who are you going to the regatta with?"

Elizabeth blinked. "Uh—I don't know."

"That's great!" Jessica said sarcastically, slapping herself on the forehead and rolling her eyes. "You have to go with someone," she added, as if this were the most obvious fact in the whole world.

"Why?" Elizabeth asked her mildly. "I'm a

reporter, Jess. Remember? Reporters don't go on dates when they're doing a story."

Jessica blinked. "I think you should go with someone who's in the race," she suggested slyly. "That way you can get kind of a bird's-eye view on the whole thing. Like—"

"Jess," Elizabeth said firmly, "I appreciate your advice. Really. But I promise, the minute I feel like I need a date I'll come straight over to the dating agency and fill out a form. But before that, consider the issue closed."

"But—"

"*Closed!*" Elizabeth exclaimed, shaking her blond head as she turned back to her book.

That's what she thinks, Jessica thought as she bounded down the hall to her bedroom. *Like it or not, I'm going to get Elizabeth and Nicholas together*, Jessica vowed. *I can see it all now. Steven will be madly in love with one of the wonderful women I found for him at the agency. And Elizabeth . . .*

Elizabeth would be the darling pet of the Morrow household. Nicholas would give her all sorts of presents and invitations, and naturally he'd think of her poor little twin sister, too! They'd probably rename one of the wings of their house the Jessica wing, out of gratitude.

These were long-range plans, and Jessica was sure they'd come to be. But right now she had her sights set on the regatta. Once Nicholas knew Elizabeth was going anyway, he'd jump at the thought of giving her a ride, Jessica thought, happily picking up the receiver of her phone and beginning to dial.

And once he and Elizabeth spent a beautiful day together at the harbor, who knew what would happen next?

Six

"I don't see what you're so nervous about," Jessica remarked. It was Tuesday afternoon, and she was sitting in a booth at the Dairi Burger across from Nicholas Morrow, fiddling with the wrapper from her straw.

"Are you really sure she wants me to call?" Nicholas asked, frowning. "Why doesn't she just call me if she really wants to see me?"

Jessica sighed impatiently. She'd never expected Nicholas to object to making a simple phone call. He'd gotten so excited when she'd called him the night before. Then suddenly his mood changed, and he insisted that Jessica meet him that afternoon for a Coke.

"I want to talk it all over with you before I call," he had told her.

Talk *what* over? Jessica had wondered. All he had to do was dial seven little numbers and

59

ask—no, *tell*—Elizabeth that he was going to pick her up on Saturday. It was simple!

"Of course she can't call you," she told him, exasperated. "She's conflicted, Nicholas! And she needs you to settle her problems. OK, maybe right now she's feeling a little low about Todd. But I can guarantee it, Nicholas. You're the one she's really crazy about. If you press it right now, I know she'll come around."

"I just felt so terrible after the last time," Nicholas said moodily. "You know how much I liked her, Jess. And I ended up falling flat on my face. If she's still in love with Todd—"

"Oh, she's not," Jessica said hastily. "Not at all. The thing is, they knew each other for such a long time, they got really used to each other! How Elizabeth felt about Todd—well, it's kind of like smoking," she concluded. "Liz couldn't help herself. She got really dependent on him, and now she's having withdrawal symptoms. But she's almost cured. And all she really needs—"

Nicholas burst out laughing. "All right, all right," he conceded. "I'll call her. Just between us," he added soberly, "I'm still awfully fond of Liz. I've thought about her a lot over the last few months, and sometimes I've considered calling her, trying again. But just looking at her and Todd. . . ." His voice trailed off. "Still, Todd's gone now," he said decisively. "It can't do any harm to try."

"That's the spirit!" Jessica cried, glancing at the clock on the wall. It was almost three forty-five, and she'd promised Mary Ann she'd be at the agency by four o'clock. "I'm going to have to run," she told him regretfully, "but thanks for the Coke, Nicholas. And good luck tonight. I'll be rooting for you."

Jessica almost burst out laughing as she hurried outside to her car. The way things were going these days, it looked as if she was going to have to make matchmaking her career!

Only one thing was bothering Jessica. She hadn't heard a single word from Steven about Beatrice Barber. Maybe he'd already fallen in love with her, Jessica thought happily, and just hadn't let anyone at home know about it yet.

But news traveled fast in the Wakefield household, and if a mysterious, glamorous older woman had called Steven up from out of nowhere, Jessica had a feeling she'd have heard about it.

She'd give her till the end of the week, Jessica told herself. And if Steven didn't mention anything when he called home, she'd have to call up one of the other two women. Steven was too good to waste.

"Hello, is this Elizabeth?" a friendly male

voice enquired. Elizabeth's heartbeat quickened when she heard the phone ring. It was nine-thirty, a little late for Todd to call, with the three-hour time difference, but maybe . . .

"Yes, it is," she said politely, trying to cover up her disappointment when she heard the unfamiliar voice. "Who is this, please?"

"Nicholas Morrow," he answered. After a brief pause, he added, "I heard that you're covering the races this weekend for *The Oracle.*"

"Yes, I am," Elizabeth said, slightly confused. "You're in the race, aren't you?" She was wondering why Nicholas was calling, but she didn't think it would be very nice to put it more directly.

"I sure am," Nicholas said, chuckling. "And if I don't get the blue ribbon, I don't know how I'm going to be able to stand it around here anymore! My father's already planning a celebration party on his boat."

Boat, Elizabeth thought, smiling, was Nicholas's understated word for the Morrows' enormous yacht. At the sound of Nicholas's voice, a flurry of memories came back to Elizabeth. She had always liked him. She didn't know him as well as his sister Regina, who was the twins' age, but she'd always seen Nicholas as a good friend—someone she could trust.

"The reason I'm calling," Nicholas continued,

"is that I wanted to know if I could pick you up and give you a ride to the marina on Saturday."

"Oh," Elizabeth said, taken aback. "That's very sweet of you, Nicholas, but—"

"Come on, Liz. I'll need a friend around to soothe my nerves before a race like that!"

"Well . . ." Elizabeth began tentatively. She couldn't see anything wrong with accepting a *ride*, though it was kind of out of the way for him. Still . . .

What happened before with Nicholas was history, Elizabeth told herself. And he knew how she felt about Todd. Nicholas was just a nice guy who happened to be racing in the regatta she was covering.

"Sure, Nicholas," she said at last. "I'd appreciate the ride. But I have to warn you," she added, "journalists are always impartial at events like this. So I don't know how much I'll really be able to soothe your nerves."

"Just having you near me should do the trick," Nicholas said lightly.

"Great," Elizabeth said and laughed. "See you on Saturday, Nicholas. And may the best man win!"

"See you," Nicholas echoed, "on Saturday."

Jessica was sprawled on the carpet in the Wakefields' living room when Elizabeth went downstairs later that evening for a glass of orange juice. "Doesn't that history book distract you from the TV set, Jess?" Elizabeth called, opening the door to the refrigerator.

Jessica rolled her eyes, flipping apathetically through her textbook. "Hey, who was that on the phone just now?" she asked nonchalantly.

"It was Steve," Elizabeth said, coming back into the room and settling down on the couch. "He told me the most amazing story! He said some woman's been calling him all week, asking him out to dinner and the movies and things like that."

"What's so amazing about that?" Jessica demanded, sitting up straight and looking attentively at her twin.

Elizabeth took a bite of the chocolate-chip cookie she'd brought in with her from the kitchen. "This woman is *old*, Jess—almost Dad's age! She's divorced, and Steven says she sounds really weird."

Jessica looked thoughtful. "Weird in what way? Did he say?"

Elizabeth burst out laughing. "Doesn't she sound weird enough already? Boy, Jess, I think this dating agency is really doing something to your judgment."

Jessica blinked rapidly. Better not let her sister dwell on the agency for very long, or she might put two and two together. "Poor Steve," she said quickly. "But I think it's kind of flattering, all the same. Do you know how she met him or anything?"

Elizabeth shook her head emphatically. "Steve's afraid he's suffering from amnesia or something. He thinks he might have met her at some party and just doesn't remember. But I know he's hoping she forgets him—and fast!"

Jessica sighed. There went Beatrice Barber down the drain, a perfectly good woman whom Steven was obviously too immature to appreciate. All she could hope now was that Jordan MacGuire or Melissa Porter would work out a little better.

"But the phone rang twice, didn't it?" she demanded suddenly. "Did Todd call?"

Elizabeth shook her head. "We promised each other we'd try to go easy on the phone for the rest of the week." She sighed. "At this rate, Todd and I are going to be indentured to the telephone company for the rest of our lives."

"So who was the other phone call from?" Jessica persisted.

Elizabeth laughed. "Have you ever thought of going to work for the FBI when you get out of school?"

Jessica sniffed. "I suppose you wish you came from a family where nobody cared what anybody else was doing?"

"Sometimes!" Elizabeth giggled. "Actually, it

was Nicholas Morrow on the phone, if you really want to know."

"Really?" Jessica asked innocently. "What did he want?"

"Nothing much. He offered me a ride to the regatta this Saturday."

Jessica looked quickly at her twin. "That's nice," she said noncommittally. "And you said yes, right?"

Elizabeth looked irritated. "As a matter of fact, I did," she replied. "But it's not really a big deal, Jessica. All he's doing is driving me to the marina and dropping me off. And that's that!"

Jessica shrugged. "Sounds fine to me," she said calmly, turning back to her history book.

"I'm going upstairs," Elizabeth said, her cheeks flushed and her eyes flashing. "If anybody wants me, tell them I'm writing to Todd!"

"OK," Jessica answered coolly, aware that her sister was upset, but pretending not to notice.

"A big long letter!" Elizabeth cried, racing from the room.

Jessica smiled to herself, flipping her textbook shut and putting her head down on her folded arms. Something was definitely going on with her twin, she thought. It seemed Elizabeth already felt guilty because she knew Nicholas still liked her. That was a good sign.

Now all she had to do, Jessica thought happily, was help Elizabeth see that *she* liked *him*, too. She'd save Elizabeth from feeling lonely and rotten—and while she was doing that she'd make her realize how much better Nicholas was for her than Todd. How much more sophisticated and exciting.

And if that wasn't being a good sister, Jessica thought, then what in the world was?

Seven

Elizabeth never would have guessed that she'd get so caught up in the suspense of the sailing races. All morning, groups had been milling around the striped tent set up on the beach, sipping drinks and exchanging excited predictions on the outcome of the regatta. Note pad in hand, Elizabeth was hurrying from the tent to the dock, trying to record as many observations as she could. The race was an annual event sponsored by the Sweet Valley Boat Club, but Elizabeth could never remember seeing so large a turnout or hearing such high-pitched speculation about who the winner would be.

"Liz! I've been looking for you everywhere!" Jessica sang out, hurrying to greet her twin from across the tent. "Where's Nicholas?" she added, dropping her voice.

Elizabeth shrugged. "I don't know. Out at the dock, probably, with all the other contestants."

"How'd it go this morning?" Jessica continued, ignoring the warning look on Elizabeth's face. "Did he—"

"Jessica," Elizabeth said firmly, "*stop being so silly. I've got to go see if I can get an interview with Mr. Davis before the races*," she added, hurrying off in pursuit of the snowy-haired chairman of the boat club.

Elizabeth couldn't believe her sister was making such a big thing out of one little ride. *It was practically on his way*, Elizabeth told herself. *And besides—*

But Elizabeth didn't have time to finish her thought. "Liz!" an aggrieved male voice called. "I've been looking for you everywhere! Don't you remember promising to help settle my nerves?"

Elizabeth spun around, her blond hair flying. "Nicholas," she said, smiling despite herself at the mock-pleading expression on his face. "I'm really sorry," she began, "but I told you I've got this story to write. If I don't get something together before this afternoon, Mr. Collins—"

"Come on," Nicholas urged, grabbing her hand. "I want you to see my boat before the race."

Several minutes later Elizabeth was at his side at the docks, looking appreciatively at the sleek, twenty-foot sailboat that had already won its sailor a good deal of acclaim. "It's lovely," Elizabeth whispered. "Does it have a name?"

Nicholas's eyes twinkled. "Two names," he told her. "One private and one public. The public name is *Seabird*. But the private name is *My Favorite Twin*," he told her, maintaining his steady gaze on her face.

Elizabeth blushed. She had no idea what to do. She knew she shouldn't let him say things like that, but she couldn't help feeling flattered at the same time. And also just a tiny bit glad that Nicholas still liked her. She'd never *do* anything about it, of course, she told herself. But there was no denying Nicholas was handsome. *And* fun. And—

"Don't tell me you're on the side of the competition!" a loud voice boomed. Elizabeth shook herself out of her reverie as Bruce Patman came bounding over, a white towel slung casually around his neck, his dark hair still wet from a recent swim.

"Hey, Morrow," Bruce continued, slapping Nicholas on the back, "I hope you don't think you're going to take me today. 'Cause just between us—"

Nicholas laughed. "Don't count your chickens, Bruce, as the old saying goes. I have a feeling today may be my best race ever."

Bruce Patman didn't suffer from lack of confidence, Elizabeth thought, grinning. The tall, good-looking senior had never been plagued by insecurity. His father was one of the richest men in Sweet Valley, and Bruce's license plate— 1BRUCE1—was a dead giveaway to his philosophy on life. The Wakefield twins had had a number of brushes with Bruce Patman, and both had decided at one point to write him off as an arrogant snob.

But Bruce had turned out to have a sensitive side, too—a side that was brought to the fore when Bruce fell in love with Nicholas's sister, Regina. A good friend of Elizabeth's, Regina was a beautiful, talented girl who had managed to make the most of life despite the fact that she was deaf. Like many of the students at Sweet Valley High, Bruce quickly forgot about Regina's handicap. And Elizabeth was so impressed with the change Regina had wrought in Bruce's behavior that she warmed toward him. Regina was in Switzerland now, undergoing treatments to restore her hearing. Elizabeth knew she and Bruce were corresponding regularly—and she also knew that the roughhousing between Bruce and Nicholas was just high-spirited fun. Like Elizabeth, Nicholas had changed his opinion of Bruce. He loved his younger sister very much, and any friend of hers quickly became a friend of his as well.

"Hey," Bruce said suddenly, giving Elizabeth

a searching look, "how're you holding up since Todd left, Liz?"

Elizabeth sighed. "It's pretty hard," she admitted. "But Vermont isn't as far as Switzerland. I'm sure you know how it feels!"

Bruce nodded. "I sure do," he told her. "And it's not a good time, I can tell you that much. Still," he added philosophically, "there's nothing like a good long love letter from time to time, right?"

"Right," Elizabeth said, laughing.

Nicholas had been listening intently to this exchange without saying a word. Suddenly he broke in, putting his hand affectionately on Bruce's shoulder. "OK, Bruce," he said, giving him a friendly shake, "what do you say we get ourselves ready to race and let Liz write her story?"

Was it her imagination, Elizabeth wondered as she made her way back up to the the tent, or had Nicholas's eyes darkened when Bruce mentioned Todd? It had to be her imagination, she told herself. And whatever the reason that she was acting so funny today, she had to cut it out. The minute the races were over, she was going straight home. And she was going to write Todd the longest, most creative love letter yet!

And she wasn't going to give Nicholas Morrow another thought.

*   *   *

Despite her impartial role, Elizabeth found herself screaming as loudly as the other spectators as two sailboats edged out in front after rounding the first buoy. She could distinguish the *Seabird* by its navy-and-white sails. The pier was crowded with spectators, jumping and screaming as the first lap of the race was completed. The contestants had to steer their boats three times around a triangular course marked by buoys. And almost as soon as the gun was fired, Bruce and Nicholas were in the lead.

"Come on, you guys," Elizabeth shouted excitedly, jumping up for a better view. "Come on!"

The second lap of the race was completed now. And the *Seabird* was edging past Bruce's fiberglass boat with the yellow trim—half a sail in front, then three-quarters of a sail—

"It's Nicholas Morrow!" Mr. Davis screamed. "He's won the blue ribbon. Nicholas Morrow and the *Seabird* have won the race!"

Elizabeth had screamed herself hoarse, and her throat was still aching minutes later when Nicholas, sopping wet after his victory dunking, pushed his way through the crowd to engulf her in an icy hug. "Come on," he said. "Remember I told you about the party my father's been planning? He wants both you and Jessica to come out on our boat with us this afternoon."

Elizabeth's head was spinning. "But I—"

73

Out of nowhere Jessica was at her side. "Way to go, Nicholas!" she cried, flinging herself happily at him.

"Jess, convince your sister to come out on our boat this afternoon," Nicholas pleaded. "You're both invited—and it won't be half as much fun without you! My dad's got a wonderful lunch planned, and—"

"Of course we'll come!" Jessica said eagerly. "Won't we, Liz? It sounds wonderful, Nicholas. But do we need to change or anything, or are we all right as we are?"

Elizabeth didn't have time to protest. In the excitement of the race's conclusion, she felt too dazed to beg her way out of the Morrows' party. Jessica seemed so positive, and it was much easier just to go along with the whole thing than to try to back out of it. Besides—

Well, why not, she found herself thinking. *I haven't done anything like this in ages. And maybe I can get some special stuff to put in the story—kind of an inside scoop.*

The afternoon proved to be really fun. Nicholas's father had arranged a catered lunch, which was superb. They even had champagne—in the middle of the day! And Nicholas was good company, relaxed, warm and attentive.

"I'm glad you came," he said softly, looking

intently at Elizabeth as he sat next to her on the starboard deck of the yacht.

"I've had a good time, Nicholas," Elizabeth admitted. "I never really congratulated you properly on winning the race this morning."

"Just do me justice in print," Nicholas instructed, smiling.

"You won't see it anyway!" Elizabeth teased him. *The Oracle* was distributed only to students at Sweet Valley High. Nicholas had graduated from high school the previous June and was working for his father's computer company that year before going on to college.

"Maybe you'll save me a copy," Nicholas said lightly.

"If the story's good," Elizabeth said and giggled. Suddenly she realized that Nicholas's expression was getting serious. Jessica was at the other end of the yacht, deep in conversation with Nicholas's cousin Jeffrey. In fact, all the Morrows were on the other side of the boat. Elizabeth and Nicholas were sitting all by themselves.

"Liz," Nicholas said quietly, dropping his gaze, "it means a lot to me that you let me give you a ride this morning. And that you came out on the boat this afternoon. I know we've never mentioned what happened between us a few months ago, but—"

"Nicholas, don't," Elizabeth said. She couldn't bear to interrupt this fun afternoon with memories. Why couldn't Nicholas just leave things as they were? She was having such a good time. . . .

Nicholas cleared his throat. "I know you miss Todd a great deal. And I don't expect to change that. I just want you to know that I'm around if you ever want someone to talk to. A shoulder to cry on, and all that. OK?"

Elizabeth breathed a great sigh of relief. So that was all! Nicholas just wanted to be her friend—nothing more!

"Hey," she whispered, impulsively squeezing his hand, "I think that's the best news I've gotten all week!"

"Liz," Nicholas said suddenly, as if he'd just remembered something, "what are you doing tomorrow afternoon?"

Elizabeth thought for a minute. *Writing to Todd*, she thought. *What else?* "I don't know," she said.

"My parents are having a barbecue, and they asked me if I wanted to invite a few friends. Maybe you and Jessica could come. It'll be mostly older people, my parents' friends, so it would be great for me if you two felt like dropping by."

Elizabeth sighed. Two days in a row, she thought uneasily. That might really be pushing her luck. But Nicholas had said that all he wanted was to be friends. And just then she really could use his company.

"Why not?" she said, flashing Nicholas a smile.

Because Todd wouldn't like it, she reminded herself. *Because we promised that we wouldn't date other people*, Elizabeth rationalized. *It'll just be a family barbecue—and Jessica will be coming with me.*

But for the rest of the afternoon Elizabeth's high spirits were suddenly—and significantly—dampened. She was having a good time with Nicholas. Almost too good.

Could she really count on the fact that Nicholas just wanted to be friends?

Eight

At first when Elizabeth woke up on Sunday morning, she couldn't remember what was wrong. She had been dreaming about Todd, and in the warm, half-conscious haze between sleeping and waking, she couldn't quite place the source of her uneasiness. Then, with a start, she remembered.

Todd wasn't there anymore. He was thousands of miles away, and it would be days before she would even hear his voice on the telephone. And his next letter wouldn't come before the next day. It was so bleak. . . .

Then, with a start, Elizabeth remembered Nicholas Morrow and the events that had taken place the day before. "And today"—she groaned and hurled herself back into her pillows—"I'm supposed to go to that barbecue at the Morrows'!"

A minute later Elizabeth was out of bed, padding barefoot over to the table, where Todd's latest letter was lying on top of a volume of poetry. With impatient eyes Elizabeth scanned the first few paragraphs of the letter in which Todd described his new school, the coach, the house in the suburbs his father had decided to buy . . .

"Here!" Elizabeth said at last, carrying the letter back to her bed and resettling herself under the blankets. She read:

Sometimes I feel really mixed up about things, Liz. There's so much I want to tell you, and even when I call, I forget half the things. I feel distant from you, but at the same time I feel as if you're with me all the time, no matter what I'm doing. I'll see something that I think would make you laugh, and I react to it as if you're right here. Does this make any sense?

It sure does, Elizabeth thought sadly, tears welling up in her eyes. She continued to read Todd's letter:

However hard it is for me, I have a feeling it must be even worse for you. At least I have the excitement—or the disruption—of a whole new place to get used to. And that sort of keeps my mind off things. But you—

The only thing that keeps me going is knowing how strong you are, Liz. But I know there are times that you won't feel strong. If you can just remember how much I love you . . .

Elizabeth bit her lip. Todd knew her so well, she thought sadly. He could imagine every mood she experienced before it even occurred. He was the best friend she'd ever had, and no matter what happened she was not going to lose him.

Elizabeth had been taken aback at the sensations she'd experienced the afternoon and evening before. The truth was that there was something very appealing about Nicholas Morrow. He was handsome, mature, sensitive, enough older than Elizabeth to seem sophisticated without being the slightest bit condescending. She would have to be inhuman not to notice that he was charming, Elizabeth admitted to herself reluctantly.

And—added to all his appeal—Elizabeth was lonely. It wasn't that she didn't have the support of a loving family or close friends to turn to. In fact, Steven had called her almost every night from college just to see how she was doing. Enid had been as good a friend as always, making sure Elizabeth was included in all her plans and looking out for her in the hallways or at lunchtime, making sure she wasn't left by herself.

But none of these things could fill the enormous vacuum left in Elizabeth's life when Todd moved. Nor did she *want* that to happen. As long as she and Todd continued to feel as they did about each other, no one could ever make that hollow place go away—no one, that was, but him.

Over the past year, Elizabeth had become used to spending much of her free time with Todd. Lunchtime, for example. They'd always been a twosome in the cafeteria. Friday and Saturday evenings were always spent together. Elizabeth remembered now hearing Enid complain about how hard it was to be on her own again after her longtime boyfriend, George Warren, broke up with her. "Sometimes I don't want to do anything!" Enid had complained. "I don't like going to dances by myself, and all my other friends have boyfriends—or at least dates. I feel like an outcast!"

Elizabeth had always told her friend that she was being silly, that she still had her friends, and that was what was really important. But now she could appreciate how Enid had felt. When Friday evening rolled around, she really didn't feel like sitting at home with her parents, watching television or reading a good book. But she didn't feel like going out with her friends, either.

Actually Elizabeth felt much better as she ran through these thoughts. It was easier for her to undersand now why she'd felt a little strange around Nicholas the previous day. "No wonder I feel funny," she said softly, folding Todd's letter. "I've been feeling terribly lonely, and along comes this great-looking guy who claims he's been attracted to me for months. What girl wouldn't want to spend time with him?" But her heart belonged to Todd, and nothing was going to change that.

Elizabeth's fingers brushed the locket Todd had fastened around her neck, and a tiny smile played about her lips. She felt a lot better after rereading Todd's letter. And now that she felt more secure about everything, she was looking forward to the barbecue at the Morrows' estate that afternoon. She was convinced that nothing Nicholas could do would change her love for Todd. Her feelings were too strong for that. And so, she knew with all her heart, were Todd's.

Jessica was in high spirits all afternoon. There was nothing she loved better than a scheme—especially one of her own invention—that was going exactly as she'd hoped. Her disappointment that Beatrice Barber hadn't worked out was more than made up for by the fact that Nicholas and Elizabeth were so obviously falling in love.

The Morrows' barbecue was being held in honor of Jeffrey, the cousin Jessica had met the previous day on the yacht. He had flown in from New York for a week's vacation in Sweet Valley. Jeffrey was twenty-one, with brown, crinkly hair and wire-frame glasses. He reminded Jessica of a librarian. Although she had considered falling in love with him for a wild moment yesterday, she had by now decided he was off limits. For one thing, Jessica knew the Morrows' wealth was all concentrated in Nicholas's family, and Jeffrey definitely struck her as a poor relation. He wanted to be an archaeologist, which had seemed interesting at first. But the more he talked about it, the dustier it began to sound.

Still, he was the reason for the party. And Jessica was so glad to be at the Morrows' that she didn't even care how much Jeffrey talked about ancient civilizations.

"Have another hot dog," Jeffrey suggested, passing Jessica the platter. They were sitting at picnic tables under the sprawling shade trees behind the back wing of the Morrows' mansion, and Jessica was trying to keep her eyes on Nicholas and Elizabeth, who were strolling together down by the tennis courts.

"Your sister seems like a very interesting girl," Jeffrey said. "Have she and Nicholas been friends for a while?"

Jessica took a huge bite of hot dog. "Ages,"

she told him, chewing. "They make a perfect couple, don't you think?"

Jeffrey turned slightly to consider the couple. "I guess so," he replied and shrugged. "Now, I was telling you about the Aztecs . . ."

Jessica did not want to talk about the Aztecs. She wanted to talk about Elizabeth and Nicholas. She wanted to try to guess exactly what they were saying to each other. Probably Elizabeth was admitting that Todd was boring and she'd always really liked Nicholas better.

But if Jessica could have heard the conversation between Nicholas and Elizabeth, she would have been very much surprised.

"How's Regina doing?" Elizabeth asked, trying not to notice how closely beside her Nicholas was walking.

"She seems fine," Nicholas answered. "We've been writing about once a week, sometimes more when she's feeling lonely. She really likes her tutor, and she's keeping up fairly well with her schoolwork. The doctors are pretty impressed with the results of her preliminary treatments. So with any luck . . ."

"It would be wonderful if she could regain her hearing!" Elizabeth said passionately.

Nicholas smiled. "It sure would."

Elizabeth looked around her at the beautifully manicured grounds of the Morrow estate. She wished she could tell Nicholas what she was really feeling. He'd been so kind to her all afternoon, rushing off to get her something to drink, asking solicitously if she wasn't still hungry. But she knew now that something strange was going on. Nicholas wasn't acting like just a friend. When his arm accidentally brushed against hers, he jerked away as if he'd been given a shock— and his face went scarlet. He listened so carefully to everything she said that Elizabeth began to feel awkward.

There was no doubt about it, she admitted to herself. He was still in love with her. It showed in everything he said and did. But what was she supposed to do about it?

"Liz, I have to ask you something," Nicholas said slowly, breaking a leaf off a low-hanging tree branch as they walked past. "Did you and Todd make an agreement about dating other people before he moved?"

Uh-oh, Elizabeth thought. *Here it comes.*

"As a matter of fact, we did," she answered slowly. "We decided it would be hard for either of us to get involved with someone else. Maintaining friendships—that's one thing." She smiled. "But anything more serious . . ."

"Does that mean I can't take you to a movie this week?" Nicholas pressed her. "There's a new James Bond movie in town. And I wondered if you would go with me. I'll have you home early," he added.

Elizabeth thought fast. She knew she shouldn't lead Nicholas on, but she'd told him the truth about Todd. And he didn't seem bothered by what she'd said.

Maybe Nicholas was a little lonely, too. It was probably hard for him, being between high school and college. And the Morrows were still new to Sweet Valley. He probably just wanted a good friend, Elizabeth told herself, just as she did. Why shouldn't she say yes?

"I'd love to go with you," she answered with a smile.

"I'm so glad," Nicholas said huskily. "I was afraid for a minute there you were going to tell me I don't even stand a chance."

"But I—"

Elizabeth didn't have a chance to answer. Nicholas turned to her suddenly, putting both hands square on her shoulders, and planted a quick kiss on the tip of her nose.

"I'm so glad," he whispered. "Elizabeth," he said, grinning, "I have a feeling this is going to be the start of a beautiful friendship!"

Elizabeth bit her lip. *He doesn't understand*, she thought anxiously. *Whatever I tell him, Nicholas doesn't seem to get it at all.*

What in the world was she going to do now?

"It's kind of a shame about Jeffrey." Jessica sighed as she followed Elizabeth into the

Wakefields' Spanish-tiled kitchen. "I mean, isn't it just my bad luck that he turns out to be interested only in bones?"

Elizabeth laughed. "He's kind of old for you anyway, isn't he?"

"Old I can handle." Jessica snorted. "What I can't handle is *ancient*. That guy's mind is back in the third century B.C."

Elizabeth opened the refrigerator and reached for the milk carton. "Did you have a good time anyway, or not?"

"It was OK," Jessica replied. "What about you?" she added slyly. "It looked like *you* had a good time."

Elizabeth shook her head. "Actually, I didn't, Jess," she told her twin. "I'm kind of worried about what's going on with Nicholas."

"Why?" Jessica asked innocently. "He's a pretty nice guy, isn't he?"

"Of course he is!" Elizabeth laughed. "You know how fond of him I am, Jess. But that's part of the problem. I'm afraid—"

"Afraid of what?" Jessica demanded, plopping down at the kitchen table.

Elizabeth turned to face her twin. "Actually, I'm afraid Nicholas may want to be more than just friends," she admitted reluctantly. "And I'm not really sure how to handle the situation."

Jessica's eyebrows shot up. "What do you

mean, 'handle' it? Why not just wait and see how things turn out?"

Elizabeth blinked. "But you see, Jess, Todd and I—"

"Todd!" Jessica burst out. "Liz, he's thousands of miles away! You can't tell me you mean to just sit around for the rest of your life, writing him letters!"

Elizabeth stared at her twin. "Not exactly. But I don't want to get involved with another guy, either. Todd and I are still very much in love. And just because we happen to be physically separated—"

"Doesn't mean you can't still mess your life up because of him," Jessica concluded.

Elizabeth shook her head. "Jess, I don't believe you!" she cried. "Why can't you understand?"

"So what are you going to do about Nicholas?" Jessica demanded. "From what I saw today, he isn't the only one thinking about something more than friendship! It looked to me like you were pretty interested, too!"

Elizabeth went pale. "As a matter of fact, I've already decided that things with Nicholas have gone far enough," she retorted. "I'm supposed to go out with him sometime this week, and I'm going to let him know that I don't think we should see each other anymore. After what happened between us the last time, I think it's just too hard to keep things natural. So I'm going to tell him we should just back off altogether."

Jessica stared at her sister. She couldn't believe her ears. How could Elizabeth make such a disastrous mistake?

It was bad enough that Elizabeth had chosen Todd over Nicholas months ago, when Todd was still around. But now . . . when Todd was no more than a voice on the telephone! It was unthinkable to Jessica, and she was determined to find some way to change her twin's mind. She would just have to save Elizabeth from herself!

Nine

It was Monday evening, and Jessica was curled up in her favorite chair in her bedroom, deeply engrossed in that month's issue of *Glamour*. As she scanned the "Dos & Don'ts," two questions kept running over and over again through her mind.

First, what in the world could she do to help Steven out, now that the mature and wealthy Beatrice Barber had been a complete failure? Maybe it was just the telephone, Jessica thought after a minute's reflection. It was so hard to get to know someone over the phone.

Steven was supposed to come home again that weekend. If she gave Jody MacGuire a call, Jessica thought rapidly, and told her to drop by the house, she was sure that would do the trick! Steven was probably just shy, and he was afraid to make the first move himself!

Jessica pushed the magazine aside, completely engrossed now in her plan. *I'll call Jody from work tomorrow afternoon,* she told herself, *and tell her to drop by Saturday afternoon. And I'm willing to bet they make a date for Saturday night!*

But that didn't help Jessica with her second, and in some ways more pressing, problem. How could she keep Elizabeth from scaring Nicholas away?

Jessica didn't have time to consider the magnitude of her task. The telephone rang, and the faint buzz inside the receiver when she put it to her ear told Jessica at once that it was a long-distance call.

"Jessica?" a familiar voice said after a moment's pause. "It's Todd. How've you been?"

If it isn't the Problem himself, Jessica thought. *I wonder if he knows what a mess he's making of my sister's social life.*

"I'm all right," Jessica said mildly. "How's Vermont? I bet it's cool there."

"It is!" Todd laughed. "Not like Sweet Valley. But it's pretty up here, Jess. I bet you'd like it."

Jessica found that unlikely, but she didn't want to hurt Todd's feelings. "I shouldn't keep you on the phone, Todd—I know it's costing a lot of money, and Liz isn't here right now."

"Oh," Todd said, obviously disappointed. "Do you know when she'll be back?"

"She's over at Enid's," Jessica said truthfully, wishing Elizabeth were out with Nicholas so she could sound mysterious. "I don't think she was expecting your call."

"No . . ." Todd said vaguely. "I was just thinking about her, and—"

Jessica fiddled with the telephone cord, an idea forming in her mind. Why not share some of her worries with Todd? If he knew what a zombie Elizabeth was turning into, if he realized that she was throwing away her *whole life* . . .

"I've been thinking about her a lot, too," Jessica said, a quaver coming into her voice. "Poor Liz."

"What do you mean?" Todd demanded. "Is anything wrong?"

"Well . . ." Jessica began. "Oh, never mind. I really shouldn't go into it now. I'm sure you know all about it, anyway."

"Know all about what?" Todd asked frantically. "Jessica, if there's something wrong with Liz that I don't know about . . ."

Here goes nothing, Jessica thought, and, she promptly burst into tears.

"Jess, what is it?"

"N-n-nothing," Jessica sobbed. "I'm sure the two of you knew what you were doing when you agreed to keep things up from so far away. I mean, you probably realize that all Elizabeth does anymore is sit around the house, writing you letters. But if that's what you *want* for her—"

"Wait a minute!" Todd exclaimed. "Back up a second, Jess. What are you trying to tell me?"

"I'm not the only one who's worried about her," Jessica said mournfully, her voice still quavering. "My parents, Steve, Enid—even Mr. Collins—everyone agrees that Liz is like another person these days. She barely sees any of her friends. She hasn't done half as much stuff for the paper. Mr. Collins practically had to force her to cover the sailing races last weekend. And as for seeming happy—well . . ."

"That's terrible." Todd moaned. "I knew she'd been writing me a lot, but I never thought—"

"I suppose it all depends on how much you really care for her," Jessica continued mercilessly, sensing she had Todd just where she wanted him. "I mean, if it were *me*, I don't think I could stand the guilt. I'd probably hang myself or something, thinking how terrible I was making her feel. But then again—"

"Jessica, you're killing me!" Todd exclaimed. "What am I supposed to do? I can't very well make my family move back to Sweet Valley, can I?"

"No," Jessica agreed. *God forbid*, she thought silently. "But you *could* just let Elizabeth go, Todd. Let her be free to make new friends—even meet new guys. Otherwise, she's going to keep burying herself in the past."

There was a long silence on the phone. "I didn't realize how much I was hurting her," Todd mumbled. "Maybe you're right, Jess."

"It's the best thing," Jessica said sympathetically, overjoyed that Todd was finally seeing the light. "However hard it is at first, I'm sure it'll all work out for the best in the long run."

After another long silence, Todd cleared his throat. "Thanks, Jess," he managed weakly. "Do me a favor," he added. It sounded like he had a big lump in his throat.

"You name it," Jessica told him, spotting the headlights of the Fiat the twins shared turning up the driveway. Elizabeth was home.

"Take care of her for me," Todd said brokenly. "Do you promise?"

"I promise," Jessica murmured, setting the receiver gently back down.

I certainly will, she thought, flinging herself down on her bed. *Between Nicholas and me, I think we'll have that department just about sewn up!*

"That's strange," Elizabeth murmured, strolling into the kitchen on Wednesday afternoon and taking an apple from the fruit bowl. "Jess, when you talked to Todd the other night, did he say anything to you about not being home much this week? I've tried him three times, and he hasn't returned my calls."

"Not a word," Jessica murmured absently, pretending to scrutinize the pink paycheck Mary Ann had given her that afternoon. "I'm just about ready to pay Mom and Dad back," she announced triumphantly. "Another week or two, and I'll be a free woman again!"

"Let's see," Elizabeth reflected, shining the apple on the front of her sweater. "He called Monday night, right? When I called him back, his mother said he was sleeping. And last night his father said he was out. I just tried again, and his mother said he wasn't there.

Jessica sighed. "Well, you know how it is, Liz. He's the new guy at school, and he's probably got a lot of social obligations. Remember what happened when Regina Morrow started at Sweet Valley High? She must have had about a million guys asking her out. Getting through to her was like reaching the president or something. Maybe—"

"You're a big help," Elizabeth said dryly. "I'm really worried about him, Jess. It isn't like Todd not to return my calls. Do you think he might be mad at me, or something?"

"How could he be mad at you?" Jessica demanded. "You've been exactly like—what's the name of that Greek woman who sat around for ten years weaving things while her husband was away?"

"Penelope." Elizabeth laughed. "Well, I don't know if that's exactly true. But I still think something weird is going on."

"He's just busy," Jessica insisted. She looked closely at her sister. "You're not getting suspicious of him, are you?"

"Of course not! I trust Todd completely, Jess, the same way he trusts me. By the way," she added casually, avoiding her sister's gaze, "if by any chance Todd calls back tonight, tell him—"

"That you're at the movies with Nicholas?" Jessica finished for her, smiling slyly.

Elizabeth turned beet red. "Jessica, don't be impossible," she cried. You know Todd would understand! Tell him—"

"Don't worry, Liz," Jessica said smoothly, patting her sister on the shoulder. "I promise! I can definitely take care of Todd, OK?"

"OK." Elizabeth sighed. She was too distraught to notice the funny expression on Jessica's face as she hurried out of the room. *There's definitely something going on*, she thought unhappily. *Todd's never been this hard to reach. Why hasn't he called me back?*

Mingled with Elizabeth's concern for Todd was an uncomfortable feeling of guilt about Nicholas Morrow. It wasn't that her behavior with Nicholas wasn't thoroughly above board.

96

She had made it clear to him that they could be no more than friends. But she knew Todd wouldn't like it. And she wasn't crazy about the situation, either.

So why should she go that night? she asked herself. Why couldn't she just call Nicholas and tell him the whole thing was off?

Because, a tiny voice inside her answered, *I like Nicholas. I've spent the last couple of weeks sitting up in my room waiting for Todd to call, or writing him letters. And I guess part of me just wants to go out and have a good time again.*

And the other part of me wants to stay right here and wait for Todd to call and tell me everything's all right, that I'm crazy to be convinced that something is beginning to pull the two of us apart.

"You OK?" Nicholas whispered, his head close to Elizabeth's in the dim exterior of the movie theater. Elizabeth could barely concentrate on the James Bond movie. She was keenly aware of Nicholas's presence beside her—the clean, fresh scent of his after-shave; his strong, supple fingers resting lightly on his knee; the handsome outline of his profile in the semidarkness.

"I'm fine," Elizabeth whispered back. But the nervous, jumpy feeling in her stomach wouldn't go away.

Elizabeth didn't think she could bear to watch

the movie to its conclusion. She knew Bond would succeed at his mission, that he'd end up stealing the woman away from her boyfriend. It was so unfair, she thought miserably. Why should things like this happen to two people in love? Why couldn't everything be simple?

"You're not OK," Nicholas said accusingly. "You're crying, aren't you?"

Elizabeth brushed impatiently at the tears that had trickled from her eyes. "I'm fine, really," she told him. "Just feeling a little nostalgic."

"Would you object if I put my arm around you?" Nicholas asked her very seriously. "It's the best way I know to offer moral support."

Elizabeth smiled through her tears. "I'd like that," she murmured. Nicholas's arm felt warm and strong around her. She didn't seem to know anymore what was right or wrong, and she settled back into the crook of his arm. Nicholas felt like a big brother to her. Somehow she felt safer with him around.

"I had a marvelous time tonight," Nicholas said later, standing on the Wakefields' front steps and smiling down at her.

Elizabeth gulped. Somehow Nicholas didn't look like an older brother right then. He looked as if he wanted to kiss her, she thought uneasily.

"I had a good time, too," she admitted.

"Liz," he whispered, leaning forward and tracing the outline of her lips with his finger. The next minute he pulled her into his arms and kissed her very gently.

At first Elizabeth didn't know what to do. Then, despite herself, she began returning his kiss, reaching up tentatively to touch the back of his neck. His mouth felt wonderful against hers, warm and tender.

Suddenly Nicholas drew away. "I'm sorry," he gasped, stepping back and looking at Elizabeth with a mixture of concern and confusion. "Liz, I wouldn't hurt you for anything in the world. You know that, don't you?"

Elizabeth nodded. "I guess I just need some time to think," she said shakily. "I'm sorry, Nicholas, but—"

"Think everything over," Nicholas said firmly. "Don't push yourself, Liz."

"Thanks for the movie," Elizabeth began. "I had a nice time, Nicholas. Honestly."

"Can I see you this weekend?" Nicholas pressed her. "Just for some ice cream or something. It doesn't have to be at night."

"Call me," Elizabeth said weakly, wishing she could turn him down right there and then.

But I like him, she thought miserably. *I like him a lot.*

Almost automatically her fingers flew up to touch the locket around her neck. "Call me," she repeated, almost stupidly, before she hurried into the house, slamming the door behind her.

She was going to have to do some serious thinking now to figure out what she was going to say to Nicholas when he did call.

Or, for that matter, what she was going to say to Todd.

Ten

By Friday afternoon Elizabeth's nerves were stretched almost to the breaking point. She still hadn't heard a word from Todd. Every time she called, either his mother or his father told her Todd was out—or busy—and said he'd get back to her. But so far he hadn't.

Even worse, his letters had stopped coming. She hadn't heard a single word from him all week. And she was beginning to lose hope.

Something she'd said or done must have upset him, Elizabeth thought miserably, letting herself in the back door of the Wakefields' house and putting her books on the kitchen counter. But what?

Elizabeth hadn't wanted to think of the only other possible explanation. But by now there seemed no way of avoiding the truth. Obviously what had happened was that Todd had gotten caught up in his new life. Maybe he'd even met a girl already. He was afraid to tell Elizabeth the truth and was trying to let her know this way.

Elizabeth felt sick when she thought of Todd with another girl. But she couldn't imagine any other reason for his avoiding her on the phone. And now that the letters had stopped coming . . . what else could it possibly be?

The strain was beginning to affect Elizabeth in a variety of ways. Her work for *The Oracle* was going downhill. Since the piece she'd done on the races, she'd barely been able to complete her "Eyes and Ears" column. She couldn't concentrate in class, either. She'd hardly been able to think of anything but Todd. Todd, that is, and Nicholas.

It wasn't like Elizabeth to lose perspective, and deep down she knew she was being unreasonable. But she couldn't help it. She missed Todd terribly, and his absence seemed to be throwing everything out of balance.

"Hey, Liz! Nicholas is here!" Jessica called, opening the door to the kitchen and looking curiously at her twin.

Elizabeth's eyebrows shot up. "Nicholas?" she gasped.

"He says he just *has* to talk to you," Jessica bubbled. "Gosh, Liz, he looks so incredibly cute!"

Elizabeth shot her twin a glare as she pushed

past her into the front hall. *I'm glad Nicholas is here,* she thought defiantly. *I'm sick and tired of sitting around waiting for Todd Wilkins. It's obvious he doesn't care one bit what happens to me anymore. And Nicholas does!*

"Liz," Nicholas began tentatively, looking nervously at her as she opened the door and urged him to come in, "I know I shouldn't have come over without calling first. But I really wanted to see you. I felt so funny about the other night, and I wanted to let you know that no matter how you feel, I want to be your friend. If it's too soon for you right now for anything else—"

Elizabeth's eyes sparkled. "Nicholas," she exclaimed, "do you have plans for this evening?"

Looking startled, Nicholas shook his head.

"How would you like to go out with me?" Elizabeth asked him, putting her hand on his arm and smiling up into his handsome face.

Nicholas stared at her. "You mean you're not upset about what happened the other night? Oh, Liz—"

"Of course I'm not upset!" Elizabeth said forcefully. "In fact," she added, taking a deep breath, "I'm really glad, Nicholas. I hope you'll give me another chance," she added, lowering her gaze.

Nicholas Morrow couldn't believe his good luck. He had been convinced that Elizabeth would never even speak to him again. And here she was, not only telling him that she wasn't angry, but actually encouraging him to stick around!

"I know a great little Italian restaurant we could go to," he said, excited.

"That sounds wonderful," Elizabeth said cheerfully. As she listened to Nicholas making arrangements to pick her up in several hours, Elizabeth tried to feel as enthusiastic as she sounded.

She just had to get used to the idea, she reassured herself. It was bound to feel a little strange at first.

But Jessica was right. Nicholas Morrow had everything. Good looks, a sense of humor, a sharp mind—and on top of all that, he was right there, not a couple thousand miles away! What more, Elizabeth asked herself almost sharply, could she possibly want?

Todd, a little voice inside her said wistfully. Plain old everyday Todd Wilkins, who had to scrimp for weeks to afford dinner in a nice restaurant. Who looked at her sideways and made everything inside her melt.

But she wasn't going to sit around forever wishing for what she couldn't have, Elizabeth told herself sternly. *Todd's in Vermont, and from what's happened this week I'm certain he doesn't want anything to do with me.*

And Nicholas Morrow was right there in Sweet Valley. And from the look on his face right then, she got the feeling he was interested.

So, Elizabeth thought, taking a deep breath—that was that. *Nicholas Morrow it is. And I'm just going to throw myself into it, and count on this stupid old heart of mine to catch up as fast as it can.*

"I'm so glad you're home," Elizabeth told her brother, propping herself up on her elbows and tilting her face back so she could feel the sun. It was Saturday afternoon, and she and Steven were out by the Wakefields' pool, enjoying the peace and quiet of a lazy weekend day. Jessica was working at the computer-dating agency that afternoon, and Steven and Elizabeth had settled themselves in for a good long talk.

"I'll be coming home next weekend, too," Steven told her. "I got a call from Lila the other day. She's having some kind of big party at her place next Saturday night, and she needs some college men around to balance things out."

"Oh, I'm so glad you're going to be there," Elizabeth told him.

Steven raised his eyebrows. "I take it that means I won't be the only Wakefield present," he teased her.

"Well, you can count on Jess to be there," Elizabeth remarked. "And I'm coming, too."

"May I ask with whom?" Steven probed gently.

Elizabeth laughed. "Go right ahead. I guess you'd know soon enough anyway, because I have a feeling I'm going to be seeing a lot more of him. I'm going with Nicholas."

Steven's brow furrowed. "Nicholas—Morrow, right?"

Elizabeth nodded. "Tall, dark, and handsome," she told him. "He looks a lot like you, in fact."

Steven snorted. "Poor guy. This is kind of a recent development, isn't it?" he continued.

Elizabeth nodded. "We've been friends for a while. But I've been seeing much more of him in the last week or two. He's so nice, Steve. I have a feeling you'll really like him when you get to know him."

"I don't doubt it," Steven said lightly. "Any friend of yours is a friend of mine. But I'm a little confused, I guess. Didn't you tell me that you and Todd had agreed not to go out with other people?"

Elizabeth flushed. "You're right. We *did* agree to that, as a matter of fact. But—"

"I don't mean to meddle," Steven went on. "If you'd rather not talk about it, that's your business. I'm just trying to keep the record straight."

Elizabeth nodded miserably. "No, I want to tell you about it, Steve. I'm not really sure *what's* going on. Nicholas has been interested in me for a while. And after Todd left he really started paying a lot of attention to me. At first I just kept telling him that it would never work. But then . . ."

"Have you talked to Todd about all this?" Steven asked gently.

Elizabeth shook her head, tears coming to her eyes. "No," she admitted. "I haven't been able to get through to him—literally." Her voice breaking a little, Elizabeth told her brother the whole story, right up to the previous night. And she had a feeling her brother understood exactly how she felt.

"It's strange about Todd," he mused, narrowing his dark eyes thoughtfully. "From what I know of him, it doesn't sound like him. I can imagine his getting caught up with new activities—even new friends. But he isn't the sort of guy who'd let things drop without talking it over."

Elizabeth sighed. "I've been through all that, Steve. I've tried and tried to invent excuses for him. But finally I just had to admit to myself that things must have changed somehow. And it won't do me any good to try to second-guess how it happened."

"Did you think about writing Todd? Telling him how confused and upset you are?"

Elizabeth shook her head. "It's no use. Things

are over between us. I'm just going to have to get used to that idea. The sooner, the better."

Steven was quiet for a minute, and Elizabeth rolled over on her stomach and stared at him indignantly. *"You're* the one who told me it was unrealistic to expect things to stay the same with Todd so far away," she reminded him. "In fact I got the distinct impression that you thought we should both plan on dating from the first."

Steven sighed. "Maybe I did feel that way a little. But you two decided something different. And what worries me is that you still haven't talked through what's happening. Until then—"

"Until then, what?" Elizabeth prompted.

Steven shook his head. "I'm just worried about *you*, that's all. I hate to see you getting yourself involved in something for the wrong reasons. I mean, if it's kind of a rebound thing—"

Elizabeth flushed hotly. "It isn't like that at all. I really like Nicholas. He's a good friend, and I enjoy being with him. It doesn't have anything to do with Todd."

Steven sighed. "Well, you know how I feel about your common sense, Liz. If it were anyone else, I really would be worried. But all the same—"

"Hey," Elizabeth said suddenly, relieved beyond measure for the interruption, "isn't that the door bell?"

Steven groaned. "Who could it be? I thought we were going to have complete peace and quiet today."

Elizabeth glanced at her watch. "It can't be Nicholas," she said thoughtfully. "He's supposed to come by this evening, and I know he would have called. Maybe—"

"Should we toss for it?" Steven asked, taking a quarter out of his pocket. "Heads you go see who it is, and tails—"

"I'll go." Elizabeth got to her feet, let herself in through the sliding door, and hurried through the house to the front hall.

But she stopped short when she opened the front door. She'd never seen anything quite like the sight that greeted her eyes. Wearing a black leather jacket and skintight leather trousers, the girl who stood there looked like someone in a movie about punk rockers. She had at least six earrings in one ear and the longest fingernails Elizabeth had ever seen.

"Uh—can I help you?" Elizabeth said, trying to conceal her shock.

The girl blinked at her, trying to look inside the house. "My name is Jody," she said. Elizabeth couldn't tell whether she had a foreign accent or a toothache. "Jody MacGuire. I'm here to see Steven."

Elizabeth repressed the desire to burst out laughing. "Why don't you come in?" she said

109

calmly, opening the door. "Steven's out at the pool." *And he's been giving me advice about whom to go out with*, she thought.

A few minutes later Jody was perched on a lounge chair, her black eyes fixed on Steven. "I must say," she drawled, "you're not *exactly* what I had in mind."

"Had in mind for what?" Steven demanded. "Who, if you don't mind my asking, *are* you? Do I know you?"

The girl lit a cigarette, throwing the match onto the patio. "I mean, my inner intuition sort of suggested you weren't right. But I thought I'd try, anyway."

"Try what?" Steven demanded. "How did you find me?"

"Look, do you know anything about Plato's theory of love?" the girl asked, drawing hard on her cigarette. Elizabeth was watching the scene before her with fascination.

"Uh—not really," Steven mumbled.

"He believes we're all trying to find our other halves," Jody said dreamily. "And that's why I'm here."

"I have a feeling," Steven said uncomfortably, "you've got the wrong house."

Elizabeth burst out laughing.

"Aren't you Steven Wakefield?" Jody persisted. "You're supposed to be my perfect match—my other half."

"OK," Steven said, getting angry. "Who told you that? How did you get my name?"

"You know," Jody said.

"No, I don't!" Steven burst out. "And would you mind just letting me know?"

"Why, through Perfect Match, of course," Jody said, looking miffed. "You really *are* kind of hung up about it, aren't you?"

"Perfect Match!" Steven and Elizabeth cried in unison, exchanging glances.

"I'm going to strangle that girl," Steven fumed, jumping to his feet. "That must explain what happened with that divorced woman last week, too!"

"Hey, what's going on here?" the girl demanded. "I'm getting all sorts of bad vibes."

"I think there's been a mistake," Elizabeth said, shaking her head and trying to suppress her laughter. Leave it to Jessica!

"She was only trying to help," she whispered to Steven as she closed the door behind Jody. "Aren't you glad to know you're part of such a concerned, loving family?"

"If I get my bare hands on her . . ."

"Bare hands on whom?" Jessica sang out innocently, throwing her purse on the counter as she came in through the back door.

"I think it's high time for me to get out of here." Elizabeth laughed and headed for the stairs. She didn't think anything she could do

111

would save Jessica's skin. When Steven was on the rampage, it was best just to let his anger run its course.

Nicholas was picking her up in less than an hour! Elizabeth had about a million things to do before he came. Hurrying into her bedroom, she checked her reflection in the mirror over her dresser, trying to decide whether or not to wash her hair.

Quite by accident, her gaze caught the glint of gold at her throat, and her fingers reached up to touch Todd's locket. Suddenly Elizabeth felt almost dizzy with sadness for what had happened.

"Oh, Todd," she murmured, her eyes filling with tears. "How in the world did we ever grow this far apart?"

And is there anything left that I can do, she thought silently, *or should I turn to Nicholas and forget that anything between Todd and me ever existed?*

Eleven

Well, well, Jessica thought, bounding angrily upstairs. *Of all the ingrates to have as an older brother.* She couldn't believe Steven hadn't liked Beatrice Barber *or* Jody MacGuire. One of them she might have been able to understand. But *both* of them—that seemed to Jessica a clear indication that her brother would rather stay at home and mope than go out and have a good time.

Anyway, at least I tried, she assured herself. *What happens to Steve now is his business.*

There was still Melissa Porter, she reminded herself, hurrying into her room and closing the door. Maybe Steven would like her.

If he didn't, Jessica didn't intend to waste one minute more on her brother's love life. The next time she looked into the files, she thought, it would be to find herself a date for Lila's party!

Lila Fowler was famous for her parties. It

wasn't just that she had her father's mansion at her disposal, or his team of servants to wine and dine her friends. She also happened to have a knack for picking the right group of people. Her parties were so good that half the fun was speculating beforehand about how she'd outdo herself this time. Helen Bradley had told Jessica the other day that Lila was going to have someone fabulous play at this one. "Her father knows some guy who manages all the biggies. That's what Caroline Pearce told me," she'd said. Jessica didn't believe it for a minute, but she knew the party would be good. And it would be a great place to have a really special date. An older man, Jessica thought dreamily, about nineteen or twenty, with a nice car. And one of those strange, glamorous names like Calvin or Montgomery or something. She was sure the computer at work could come up with something.

Kicking her shoes off and throwing herself across her bed, Jessica began to dial Lila's number. One of the worst things about her part-time job was that it made her have to work double-time to catch up on all the gossip. It was almost six, and Jessica wanted to find out what was going on that night. And Lila was a pretty good place to begin, especially now that Cara was so withdrawn.

"Come on over tonight," Lila urged when she

heard Jessica didn't have any plans. "I'm making the final guest list for my party, and I'm trying to decide if we should have a theme or not."

"What sort of theme?" Jessica asked doubtfully.

"My cousin had a wonderful theme party after she had her appendix out," Lila said and giggled. "It was a post-op party, and everyone had to dress 'hospital.' And she turned up wearing one of those gowns that don't close in the back. It was hilarious."

Jessica couldn't imagine anything less romantic than having to dress up like a thermometer or something. "Lila, I think you need my planning powers," she told her friend. "I'll be over right after dinner."

"Hey, what's the deal with Liz?" Lila demanded. "Am I supposed to assume Nicholas Morrow isn't available anymore? He was on my list of eligible guys."

Jessica laughed. "Better cross him out, Lila. He and Liz seem inseparable these days."

"That was quick," Lila observed. "It's kind of on the rebound, don't you think?"

Jessica thought for a minute. "I think Nicholas is a big improvement over Todd. That's what I think."

"And Liz?" Lila prompted. "Does she think so too?"

"You haven't seen her holding back, have

you?" Jessica demanded. "They've had about three dates this week. And from the way it sounds, they're going to be together almost every day this coming week. They're going out for dinner again tonight. Tomorrow Nicholas is taking Liz horseback riding. What else? . . . Oh, she's going up to the Morrows' house for dinner sometime next week. Get this. Nicholas says he wants to take her *star-gazing*. Can you believe that?"

"What does Todd think of all this?" Lila asked.

Jessica was quiet for a minute. "Who knows?" she said airily. "To tell you the truth, Lila, I don't even think they're talking very much anymore. I think their little thing just sort of took its natural course and died."

"Hmmm," Lila mused. "It didn't seem like it would be that way when he was leaving. The night Enid had that party for Todd at the Beach Disco—"

"Oh, *that*," Jessica said hastily. "Well, Lila, you know how it is. Things get really romantic when you're saying good-bye. But now that the dust has settled—"

"Still," Lila said, "I find it kind of surprising. I never really thought of your sister as the fickle type, really. I guess—"

"People change," Jessica concluded. "Who knows? Liz never really seemed like a real woman-of-the-world, but I think once Todd moved she had to wake up and face the truth. I mean, she found herself completely on her own. Nicholas looks pretty good under ordinary circumstances. But when you think how lonely she must have been—"

"Love on the rebound," Lila repeated. "I bet it lasts about a week."

Jessica sniffed. "You just don't recognize true love when you see it, Lila."

"Maybe not." Lila laughed. "I guess I just don't have your professional expertise. But whatever you say, I'm going to stick to my prediction. I'd even be willing to make another bet with you—that within a week, or two weeks at the very most, Elizabeth tells Nicholas to get lost forever."

Jessica had lost one bet with Lila already, and the consequences had been grave enough to keep her from taking her friend on again. "Just wait and see," she said mildly. "Whatever you think right now, Lila, Nicholas and Elizabeth are falling madly in love with each other. And it looks to me like that's the way things are going to stay!"

It was Tuesday afternoon, and Elizabeth and Enid were lying on striped towels on the beach, listening to the waves crashing over the rocks. School had let out less than half an hour before, but already Elizabeth felt as relaxed as if it were the middle of summer.

"This is one of my favorite things about living in Sweet Valley," Enid said, rubbing suntan lotion on her calves. "Can you imagine coming out of school and having it be freezing cold? It would be awful."

Poor Todd, Elizabeth thought suddenly. *I bet it's still cold so far north.*

Every once in a while a quick flash of memory came to Elizabeth. But she tried to push it from her mind. Wherever Todd was right now, she was certain he wasn't thinking of her. And if he was, why hadn't he written? Or answered her calls?

"Sunday afternoon was so much fun," she said quickly, trying not to dwell on something she couldn't change. "Nicholas took me riding on this farm way out in the country. He's a really good rider, Enid. He's won blue ribbons in shows all over the country. And he says he can teach me how to jump!"

Enid's green eyes narrowed. "You've been spending an awful lot of time with him lately, haven't you?" she said lightly. "I feel like I was really lucky you could squeeze me in this afternoon!"

Elizabeth blushed. "Oh, Enid, you know I always have time for you!" she exclaimed, reaching out to give her friend a quick hug. "I

118

have been seeing a lot of him," she admitted. "More than I guess I really expected. But I have such a good time with him, Enid."

Elizabeth hadn't told Enid that Todd had stopped writing or calling. She was too deeply hurt to tell anyone about it. She imagined her family knew the truth, though Steven was the only one she'd spoken to about it. But no one at school knew what had happened.

"You know," Enid was saying thoughtfully, "I remember how terrible I felt when George left me for Robin. I was so depressed, Liz. I just felt like I couldn't function without him—or without a boyfriend. I mean, I was so used to always having a date on Friday and Saturday nights, always having someone around who loved me. My first impulse was to find some other guy, *fast*. As if I could replace George or something. And I sort of tried. But you know—"

"I know what you're thinking," Elizabeth said defensively. "You think I'm using Nicholas as a substitute for Todd, that I'm just spending time with him because Todd isn't here. But that isn't true at all. I like Nicholas, Enid. It isn't a rebound sort of thing at all."

Enid sighed. "It's just that it all happened so fast," she said gently. "I'm kind of worried about you. And I don't think I'm the only one, either. It seems that one minute there was Todd, and you were swearing you'd never go out with anyone else, and now all of a sudden there's no one but Nicholas. It isn't like you, Liz."

Elizabeth bit her lip. First Steven, now Enid. They both thought she was making a mess of things.

But she wasn't! She really wasn't. Todd was a thing of the past, and the sooner she really got that through her head, the better off she'd be.

But why did Enid and Steven feel she was doing something wrong? Except for Jessica, no two people in the world knew her as well, or cared for her as much. And both Steven and Enid seemed convinced that she was fooling herself, that what she thought she felt for Nicholas wasn't genuine.

Were they right? Elizabeth worried. Was she using Nicholas as a substitute for Todd? Or was he really, despite what everybody else seemed to think, the one for her, the boy she'd been waiting for all her life?

Elizabeth didn't know. And she had no idea how she was going to find out.

It was Friday afternoon, and Elizabeth was walking home from school. Jessica had offered her a ride, but Elizabeth had a lot on her mind and wanted to be alone.

Though it was a gorgeous afternoon, Elizabeth barely noticed the sun on her arms or the beautiful green of the lawns and trees around her. She

120

was remembering the first time Todd had taken her in his arms. Elizabeth had never felt a kiss as soft as Todd's, or a touch as gentle.

He can't just have forgotten me, Elizabeth thought miserably. *He just can't have!*

Over the last day or two Elizabeth had been carefully weighing what Steven and Enid had said to her. And she had come up with a painful decision. She wasn't in love with Nicholas Morrow, even though she had tried to convince herself she was. Deep in her heart she was still in love with Todd. And until she resolved things with him, she would never be ready to move on to someone else. She was going to have to find a way to get through to him—somehow.

And as for Nicholas . . . well, Nicholas would have to be told. Elizabeth could see why she'd been so attracted to him, but she knew her reasons were the wrong ones. In her initial loneliness and confusion, he had been a stronghold, a rock, someone to hang onto. And, as Enid had suggested, he had in some sense been a replacement for Todd.

Elizabeth realized that she wasn't ready to get seriously involved with another guy, no matter what Todd said if and when she could get through to him. Todd was far away, and she was going to have to face that—alone.

Elizabeth had always prided herself on her independence. Other girls got so wrapped up in

121

their boyfriends they completely lost their identities. She had seen that recently with DeeDee Gordon and Bill Chase. But Elizabeth, despite her closeness with Todd, had always maintained separate interests—like writing for *The Oracle*. Part of what made it so special between her and Todd had been that each had brought separate ideas and experiences to the relationship.

Elizabeth could see now that her independence had in part depended on Todd's being around for her whenever she needed him. Because when Todd left, she had sort of fallen apart. Without him to lean on, she had begun to ignore the things that mattered most to her—her friends, her classes, her work for the newspaper. She'd acted as if she couldn't get along without someone, a boyfriend, to bolster her up.

Realizing this now, Elizabeth felt deeply ashamed of her behavior during the previous week or two. To begin with, she had hidden herself away, spending all her free time writing or calling Todd. She had been unable to strike a balance between maintaining her affection for him and continuing her life in Sweet Valley. And then Nicholas had come along, and Elizabeth had fallen for him—hard and fast. She'd transferred a good deal of the affection she'd felt for Todd onto him. And in this way she'd denied that she still had deep feelings for Todd, feelings that would have to be dealt with openly, not hidden away.

As she got closer and closer to home, Elizabeth's mind began to clear. What she had to do seemed obvious to her now. First, she would write to Todd as Steven had suggested. She wouldn't tell him about Nicholas, but she would tell him how confused and upset she'd been by his sudden silence. And she would ask him to let her know exactly what was going on.

In the meantime she would have to tell Nicholas her true feelings. What hurt Elizabeth more than anything was the recognition that her behavior had hurt someone other than herself. Nicholas really cared for her, and it was going to be a terrible blow when he found out that Elizabeth wanted to cut things off.

But I've got to do it, Elizabeth resolved, *and the sooner the better.*

Unfortunately, Nicholas was going out with his parents that night and wouldn't be back home until very late. And his father was taking him out on the yacht the next afternoon. He had agreed to pick Elizabeth up at about eight o'clock the following night and go with her to Lila's party.

She could hardly break the date with him with such little notice, Elizabeth thought unhappily. It looked as if they'd have to go to Lila's party together as they'd planned. And that meant she'd have to wait until after the party to tell him about her decision. She'd promised to go with him, and it didn't seem fair to spoil the whole evening by telling him sooner. But the longer she put it off, the harder it was going to be.

Twelve

"It's strange," Todd Wilkins murmured to himself as he turned his father's car down the familiar streets of Sweet Valley. "It's the same old neighborhood, but it feels so different!"

No one but the Egberts knew that Todd was in town for the weekend. He had flown in from Vermont late the previous night, and that day, Saturday, he had been running errands for his father, making enquiries about the furniture, closing the family account at the bank. His father had intended to make the trip with Todd, but at the last minute had been too wrapped up in business. So Todd had come alone.

His first thought, of course, was of Elizabeth. He had worried all week long about whether or not he should call her, and had finally decided to drop by her house instead and surprise her. Todd still couldn't sort out how he felt about what Jessica had told him several weeks earlier on the phone. He had never before had to face this kind of guilt. From what Jessica told him, it sounded as though he were ruining Elizabeth's life. Maybe he should have answered her phone calls so they could talk things over. But he'd been afraid that he couldn't hold out once she knew the truth. Suppose she still wanted to be his girlfriend, even after he'd confronted her with what Jessica said?

No, he'd decided it was better this way—the hard way. He knew Elizabeth was probably confused and angry, maybe even furious. But he hoped that would help her get over him. *I'm doing it for her*, he reminded himself, turning the car down the street where the Wakefields lived. *It's been horrible for me, too. But it's the only way.*

Todd hadn't expected Jessica's words to make so great an impression on him. Maybe his parents' concern had already made him touchy about Elizabeth's freedom. In any case, he felt he had been wrong to agree not to date other people. Not that he'd met anyone in Vermont, or even that he'd wanted to. No, Elizabeth was it for Todd; he was convinced of that. But he had accepted the fact that he'd be away from her a long time—over a year, if not longer. And how often would he be able to come and visit? Every couple of months, if that! What kind of life would that be for her? What was she supposed to do between visits—sit and write him letters?

Todd had decided the distance was too great for now. He had convinced himself that the only way to help Liz get over him was to cut off communication completely. Or so he had thought until this weekend.

As the time for his visit grew closer, Todd found himself thinking about Elizabeth more and more. She was constantly in his thoughts anyway, but the prospect of being in Sweet Valley—of actually seeing her—was so exciting that he could barely contain himself. He thought about calling her to let her know that he'd be in town. But he kept himself from doing so, convinced it would be the wrong move.

And now here he was, driving past her house in the Ebgerts' car, his heart in his throat. What would it be like to see her? Would she forgive him for his behavior—and more important, understand why it had happened?"

Todd couldn't believe it, but his fingers were actually trembling. "I can't do it," he whispered, his throat dry. "I'm too frightened to go up to the door."

Winston had told him that Lila Fowler was having a party that night, and Todd was sure Elizabeth would be there. "I'm too much of a coward to face her alone," he admitted. "Maybe tonight, with plenty of people around, it'll be easier just to run over to her and give her an enormous hug."

"I'll tell her tonight," Todd whispered, putting his foot on the gas pedal. "I'll take her in my arms and explain everything that happened, from the very beginning.

"And maybe, just maybe, she'll forgive me, and tell me she still loves me as much as I love her."

It was late Saturday afternoon, and Steven Wakefield was driving down the highway, two exits before Sweet Valley. He'd left his dorm later than he planned, and he knew he'd have to hurry if he wanted to make it home in time for dinner before Lila's party. Not that he was that excited about going. Most of Lila's guests would be younger than he, and he really wouldn't have minded missing it. But he was worried about Elizabeth and this thing with Nicholas. The party would be a good chance to see what was *really* going on.

Besides, he'd invited Betsy Martin and Jason Stone to go along. He hadn't seen Betsy for a while. She'd been away for a few weeks and had just arrived back in town the previous day. Betsy was older than Tricia and at one point had gotten herself into a lot of trouble. But Steven knew she was a good person at heart. Her new boyfriend, Jason, who went to college with Steven, had helped—as Steven had—to encourage her interest in art. Betsy was slowly getting it all together.

Suddenly Steven was distracted from his thoughts as he noticed a car at the edge of the highway about a hundred yards in front of him. A girl was crouching behind it, examining the back tire, which appeared to be flat. Steven honked the horn, slowing down and signaling as he pulled off onto the shoulder of the road. *She could get killed,* he thought. *She should have that car completely off the road. She's liable to get hit where she is!*

A minute later Steven was out of his car and approaching the stalled car. "Hey," he called, "can I be of any help here?"

"Steve!" the girl exclaimed, straightening up and rubbing a smudge of grease from her nose. "Oh, thank God you're here! I've got a flat tire, and I have absolutely no idea what to do with it!"

It was Cara Walker—just about the last person Steven would have expected to run into on Route 29. Somehow he'd always gotten the impression that Cara was incapable of driving to the supermarket, let alone taking a car out on the expressway.

Within minutes Steven had moved the car off the edge of the road onto the shoulder. Luckily Cara had a jack in her trunk, as well as a spare tire, and Steven changed it for her easily. "Now, be sure to get your tire fixed right away," he admonished, wiping his hands on a rag to get the grime off them. "And next time, take the car completely off the road!"

Cara shook her head. "Thanks, Steve," she said quietly. "I guess I wasn't really paying attention. I've had a lot on my mind these days, and—"

Tears glistened in her brown eyes, and Steven felt a rush of sympathy for her. He'd never thought Cara was so vulnerable. He had always thought she was like most of the girls Jessica hung around with. But she seemed so different now. . . .

"Hey," Steven said suddenly, all thoughts of dinner forgotten, "how would you feel about a cup of coffee? If you get in your car and drive to the next exit, I'll follow you. There's a place called the Whistle Stop that isn't bad. You look like you could use a friend to talk to."

"I'd love to," Cara said gratefully.

Ten minutes later they were facing each other in a narrow booth, coffee steaming in their mugs. "I was on my way home from the family counselor's office this afternoon," Cara told him, fiddling with her coffee spoon. "And I think I was kind of upset."

She proceeded to fill Steven in on what had happened at home—the long, tense weeks when her parents were trying to decide whether or not to stay together and the loneliness she felt now that they'd separated.

"And the very worst," Cara concluded, "is that my parents decided to split Charlie and me up. He's only thirteen, and he is so vulnerable. But he's gone to Chicago with Daddy, and I'm staying here with my mother. It's terrible. I miss him so much—both of them so much. . . ."

Steven couldn't get over the change in Cara. The tragic battle that had been waged in her household had had one positive effect: Cara had grown up. Gone was the spoiled, silly girl Steven had once known. In her place was a sensitive, intelligent young woman, whom Steven thought he wouldn't mind getting to know better.

"I've talked so much about myself," Cara said shyly, looking down at her cup. "What about you, Steven? What are you doing back in Sweet Valley today?"

"I'm home for a party," Steven told her. "In fact, I was about to ask you about it. Are you going to Lila Fowler's tonight?"

Cara shook her head. "I wasn't going to," she admitted. "I've been kind of hanging out around the house these days. But maybe . . ."

"I'd like it if you'd come," Steven said gently.

A slow smile spread over Cara's face. "OK!" she said suddenly. "I will."

"I'll be looking forward to seeing you," Steven told her. And with a start, he realized that he meant it. For the first time in months—since Tricia's death, in fact—Steven was looking forward to seeing a girl again.

I think, he thought with a smile, reaching in his pocket for his wallet, *that we have some things in common. Cara and I—we're both victims in a way. I'm still torn up over Tricia's death; she's torn up over her parents' divorce and the loss of her brother.*

Maybe, he thought—*just maybe—we can help each other back on the road to recovery.*

Jessica was having a hard time avoiding her date, despite the fact that Lila's party, themeless after all, was in full swing and there were hundreds of people milling around the lawn. His name was Spence Millgate—romantic, Jessica had thought the previous afternoon at work. But he'd turned out to be an unbelievable creep. For one thing, he didn't look the tiniest bit like the photo he'd sent in with his application. He was terribly scrawny, and he was wearing enormous spectacles that made him look like a raccoon. His application claimed he was interested in sports, movies, and "having a good time." But within five minutes of meeting him, Jessica had found out that he wanted to become an undertaker when he got older. "Embalming is a fascinating subject," Spence told her, looking ghoulishly at Jessica.

Jessica needed no more than one glance at

Spence to decide that she'd had it with the Lonely Hearts agency. She'd saved a hundred and fifty dollars, and when she subtracted what she'd spent on the dress she was wearing that night, she'd have just enough to pay her parents back.

"I got nothing but aggravation out of the place," Jessica fumed, hurrying across the lawn in search of Cara or Lila—anyone but Spence Millgate. Even Melissa Porter had proved to be a disaster. Jessica had spent an entire hour trying to track her down to see if she could come to Lila's party and surprise Steven. But Melissa had chickened out. "I've decided I prefer food to men," she'd told Jessica on the phone.

"So much for fixing people up," Jessica murmured. "What a complete disaster." Her eyes brightened as she caught sight of Nicholas and Elizabeth across the garden. Her twin looked radiant, she thought. Nicholas looked more handsome than ever in a pair of white linen slacks and a striped cotton sweater. *At least I succeeded with the two of them*, Jessica congratulated herself silently.

In her haste to escape from Spence, Jessica accidentally bumped into a girl whose back was to her. "Excuse me," Jessica said automatically, about to hurry on.

The girl spun around, an irritated expression

on her face. "Oh, Jessica," she said, the frown lines deepening around her mouth. "It's *you*."

"Betsy Martin!" Jessica exclaimed. "What are you doing here?"

"Your brother asked me," Betsy snapped.

After Tricia had died, Steven had convinced his family to take Tricia's sister Betsy in. Mrs. Martin had died years before, and Mr. Martin had disappeared on a drinking binge when Tricia had become seriously ill. Betsy felt she owed a great deal to Steven. He had helped her to get over her sister's death, and more than that, he'd taken her away from the bad crowd she'd been hanging around with and had introduced her to Jason. Because of Steven and Jason's encouragement, she had won a scholarship to art school, where she would be starting in the fall.

Jessica had never liked Betsy, but she had to admit she had improved. That night she almost looked respectable in a blue dress and high heels—not shabby and cheap as she used to, Jessica thought.

"What's wrong?" Jessica asked, suddenly noticing the angry expression on Betsy's face.

"Nothing," Betsy said shortly. "I guess I just didn't expect your brother to be carrying on with someone else so soon after Trish—" Her voice broke, and Jessica narrowed her eyes, trying to follow Betsy's stare.

Sure enough, there was Steven, deep in conversation with Cara.

"Oh, Betsy!" Jessica said, laughing. "Don't be silly! That's only Cara Walker!"

"I don't care *who* it is," Betsy said sullenly, turning on her heel. "I think it's pretty low of Steven. And if I get a chance, I'm going to let him know how I feel."

"Betsy—" Jessica began. But the word died on her lips. She had just caught sight of something that almost made her hair stand on end, and her eyes widened in disbelief as she watched what could only be a ghost making his way across the lawn of Fowler Crest.

But ghosts don't wear blazers and cords, Jessica thought hysterically. *I've got to find Liz!*

In her haste to get to the pavilion where she'd last seen her sister, Jessica almost fell down. The grass was slippery with dew, and her heels were high enough to make running impossible. "It can't be Todd," Jessica gasped under her breath. "What in God's name is he doing here?"

"Jessica!" Todd called, quickening his steps to match hers. "Where are you rushing off to? Don't I even warrant a hello?"

"I—uh—Todd, what are you doing here?" Jessica gasped.

Todd smiled. "Just came back to visit the old haunts," he joked. "Hey, where's Liz?"

Jessica caught her breath. "Well, as a matter of

135

fact, I was just looking for her, Todd. I think she's in the pool."

"Is that why you're running as fast as you can toward the pavilion?" Todd asked. "Come on, Jess. Don't hold out on an out-of-towner. Where is she?"

Jessica gulped. "I don't know, Todd. I honestly don't. But before you go try to find her, I think there's something . . ."

Jessica didn't have time to finish her sentence. She and Todd had made it close enough to the pavilion now to see the dance floor, illuminated by floodlights. And from the look on Todd's face, Jessica realized it was too late for a warning.

Following his gaze, Jessica saw what had made the color drain from Todd's face. It was Elizabeth, pretty as an angel in a cream-colored dress, her blond hair gleaming as the light hit it. Her eyes were closed dreamily, and her head was resting on Nicholas Morrow's shoulder. She was dancing in his arms, seemingly oblivious to the whole world. But the next second her eyes flew open, as if she sensed she was being watched.

"Todd!" she screamed, pushing Nicholas away. There was a look of confusion and horror on her lovely face. "Todd!"

Her single syllable reverberated in the stunned silence around her—and Todd spun on his heels and raced away into the darkness.

Thirteen

"It's no use." Elizabeth wept, turning away from Nicholas's troubled gaze. "He's gone."

"You're trembling," Nicholas said softly, putting his arm around her shoulders.

Elizabeth's breath caught in her throat. "Nicholas," she said pleadingly, "will you take me home? I think I need to be by myself for a while." There was no sense in trying to explain to Nicholas what she was feeling right now: the shock of seeing Todd, the sympathetic ache she had felt when she saw the look of painful recognition on his face, and the humiliation of being watched by all her friends. Two thoughts were racing wildly through Elizabeth's head. She wanted to get out of there, away from those staring eyes; and she wanted—no, *needed*—to find Todd.

"You're really shaken up," Nicholas observed

quietly when they were alone in his car. "What is it, Liz? Was it the shock of seeing Todd again? Or is it more than that?"

Elizabeth stared dully at the dashboard before her. "Nicholas, I owe you an apology," she murmured. "An apology as well as an explanation. I was planning to tell you this tonight anyway, but seeing Todd really brought it home to me. I'm just not ready to be involved with you. There's still too much feeling left in me for Todd. And, Nicholas, until I resolve that—"

Nicholas's face went taut. "I was afraid you'd say something like that," he muttered, turning the key in the ignition.

Elizabeth sighed. What a mess she'd made, she thought miserably. But she just had to get things out in the open. She had to face how she really felt.

"I tried, Nicholas," Elizabeth said, weeping, her face in her hands. "But I'm just not ready yet. You know how much I care for you. You're a wonderful friend, and I don't know how I'd have gotten through the last few weeks without your support. But . . ."

"But you're still in love with Todd," Nicholas finished for her. "I can see it in your eyes."

"I don't know," she whispered. "I think maybe I am. But, Nicholas, what matters most is that I find a way now to stand on my own two feet. Todd just can't be around for me anymore.

And I can't expect you to take his place. I have to learn how to take care of myself."

Nicholas sighed. "Well, Liz, I think you know how I feel about you. I haven't stopped loving you since the day I met you. And what you're telling me now doesn't change the way I feel. I guess all I can do is give you more time, let you think things through . . ."

"No, Nicholas," Elizabeth said firmly. "I can't let you do that. I've been weak enough lately as it is. You have to believe me. I can't be anything more than your friend. If you still want that, that is. . . ."

Nicholas's jaw was clenched as he drove. "Of course I do!" he told her. "Liz, I feel so strongly about you. If you just want to be friends, so be it. I'll take you at your word this time and leave it at that. But you can't treat me like a yo-yo, either. If you just want to be friends, you're going to have to stick to that. Because I don't think I'll ever have the guts to try to make you love me again."

Elizabeth could barely stand looking at Nicholas's face. *He's been so wonderful to me,* she thought painfully, *and I've treated him horribly. If I let him go now,* she told herself, *I'll never get another chance.*

Nicholas pulled his car up into the Wakefields' driveway and stared straight ahead. Part of Elizabeth yearned to fling herself into Nicholas's arms and let herself be comforted. He seemed so strong, so secure. But at the same time Elizabeth knew she had to do the right thing, she had to follow her heart.

Somewhere out there the boy she really loved was hiding. And until she found him, Elizabeth knew she'd never rest another minute, her whole life long.

"I'm sorry, Nicholas," she sobbed. "Please forgive me!"

The next minute she was out of his car, stumbling toward the Wakefields' front door. Never in her life had she seen an expression as hurt as Nicholas's when she left him then.

Except, she remembered, *the look on Todd's face when he caught sight of me dancing in another boy's arms.*

Jessica could barely believe the commotion at Lila's party after Nicholas took her sister away. Everyone was buzzing about what they'd seen—Todd's sudden appearance, the pained look on his face, and Elizabeth's dramatic reaction.

"Boy, how romantic!" Lila said smugly. Jessica could tell Lila thought her sister and Todd's theatrics were a free bonus entertainment for her guests. But Jessica didn't have time to tell her friend to quit being obnoxious.

She had to get home, she thought anxiously, scanning the crowd for Spence Millgate, who had driven her to the party. It hadn't occurred to

Jessica that Elizabeth and Todd might see each other before she had a chance to explain to her twin what she'd told Todd. If Elizabeth found him and he told her what Jessica had said that night on the phone . . .

Jessica couldn't bear to think of the consequences. She had meddled in her sister's life often enough before, but never to this extent— and never with such serious effect. *None of this would have happened if it weren't for me*, Jessica thought nervously, cursing Spence Millgate for having disappeared the one time she needed him.

In the end Jessica had to borrow one of the Fowlers' cars to get home. Spence was nowhere to be seen.

"Boy, you and Liz are really making dramatic exits tonight," Lila observed wryly. But Jessica barely noticed. All she could think about was getting home in time to tell Elizabeth what she'd done before Todd found her—or Elizabeth found Todd.

She had a feeling she didn't have a minute to lose.

"I don't understand," Elizabeth said dully, splashing cold water on her tear-streaked face. "You said *what* to Todd?"

Elizabeth had changed into jeans and a sweater, and her dress was lying crumpled on

141

the bathroom floor. Jessica had never seen her twin in such a state.

"I was really only trying to help, Liz," she said nervously. "I was so worried about you. All you seemed to be doing was sitting around and writing Todd letters. So when he called, I sort of—"

"Told him to leave me alone," Elizabeth finished for her. "Is that right?"

Jessica blinked. "Liz, you've got to understand!" she said desperately. "I really had your best interests in mind. And I didn't really *tell* Todd anything. He just sort of came to that conclusion, I guess. And—"

Elizabeth stared at Jessica, but her eyes didn't seem to be focusing. "Jess, let's talk about this later," she said suddenly. "If anyone wants to know where I am, tell them I'm still at the party, OK?"

"Where are you going?" Jessica wailed, hanging over the railing as her sister bounded downstairs.

"Out for a drive!" Elizabeth hollered back as she headed out of the house.

Elizabeth was amost ready to give up. She'd been almost everywhere—to the Dairi Burger, past the school, even up to Miller's Point. She'd driven past every place Todd used to go when he was upset, or just wanted to think. To make matters worse, she didn't even know where Todd was staying. At the Egberts'? At a hotel with his parents?

Her hands were clenched tightly on the steering wheel as she drove, her eyes glued to the road. But while she was paying attention to her driving, her mind was racing with what Jessica had told her. *No wonder,* she thought furiously. *He stopped answering my calls because he thought the only way to save me was to let me go. How could he know that Jessica was stretching the truth? He did what he thought was best. And when he came back here, what did he find—me in Nicholas's arms! He must think I never loved him, if I could get over him so quickly. He must be so miserable, so angry with me. . . .*

Finally Elizabeth had to admit that she couldn't find him. "It's like looking for a needle in a haystack," she muttered, turning the car around in a driveway and heading back home. She could never remember feeling quite so sad before in her whole life.

On a whim, Elizabeth turned the Fiat down the side street where the Wilkinses' house was. The street was dark and deserted. Parking the car on the street, Elizabeth got out and cut across the Wilkinses' lawn to the backyard. It took several minutes for her eyes to grow accustomed to the darkness. "Todd . . ." she said tentatively, stepping forward toward the dark shape sitting huddled up on the lawn. "Oh, Todd . . ."

143

The next minute they were in each other's arms. Neither was able to speak, they were so busy kissing each other. Elizabeth was crying, and so was Todd. "I've been looking for you everywhere," she sobbed. "Oh, Todd, thank goodness I found you."

"Liz," Todd said brokenly, pushing her hair back so he could look into her eyes. "You're trembling," he said, pulling her closer. "Come on," he added, getting to his feet and pulling her up with him. "Let's go to the car. I think you and I need to have a long talk."

An hour later Elizabeth and Todd were still talking, holding each other's hands inside the Wakefields' red Fiat. "You see, it wasn't really Jessica's fault," Elizabeth concluded. "I don't think we were able to talk things through before you moved. And I guess I kind of snapped once you were gone. I thought our relationship had to be all or nothing. And when I didn't hear from you, I assumed you didn't love me anymore."

"I don't blame Jessica," Todd said slowly. "And I don't blame you for what happened with Nicholas, either. Let's face it, Liz. We're going to be apart for a long, long time. Who knows how long it'll be before I can come back for another weekend? And until then—"

"We both need to make our own separate lives," Elizabeth concluded for him. "But that doesn't mean I'm going to stop loving you."

144

"Me, neither," Todd whispered, leaning forward to kiss her on the lips. "All I can tell you is this, Liz: I think we've got to let our hearts be our consciences. But after the last month, I'd never tell you you shouldn't go out on dates. I just can't be responsible for restricting your freedom like that. I want you to make as many new friends as you can. And at the same time, I'm going to hope like mad that when I see you again . . ."

"Oh, Todd." Elizabeth threw her arms around him. "I love you so much!" Then she pulled away and touched the locket at her throat. "I never took this off, you know," she told him. "And I have a feeling I never will."

"Good," Todd whispered, lacing his fingers through hers. "As long as you realize that it's a token of friendship, and not a chain, then I can't imagine a better place for it to be."

A long time later, Elizabeth drove into the Wakefields' driveway. She sat in the car thinking. She still couldn't believe the sequence of events that evening. And Todd was really there, she thought gratefully. She'd get to see him for the entire next day before he left for Vermont.

Now she had a score to settle with Jessica—although she couldn't help feeling almost grateful to her twin. Jessica had been able to see what Todd and she couldn't, she told herself. That they both needed to get themselves back on their own two feet. That they couldn't just deny what had happened.

I wouldn't feel this way if things hadn't worked out in the end between Todd and me, Elizabeth admitted as she got out of the car. *But since they did, maybe I can let Jessica off with a warning, instead of a full-scale attack of sibling revenge!*